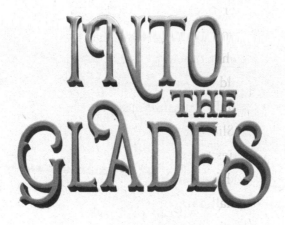

Also by Laura Sebastian

FOR YOUNG ADULTS

THE ASH PRINCESS SERIES

Ash Princess

Lady Smoke

Ember Queen

Castles in Their Bones

FOR ADULT READERS

Half Sick of Shadows

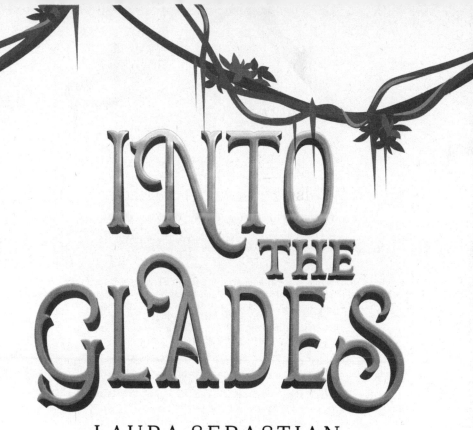

INTO THE GLADES

LAURA SEBASTIAN

DELACORTE PRESS

Text copyright © 2022 by Laura Sebastian
Jacket art copyright © 2022 by Vivienne To

All rights reserved. Published in the United States by Delacorte Press, an imprint of Random House Children's Books, a division of Penguin Random House LLC, New York.

Delacorte Press is a registered trademark and the colophon is a trademark of Penguin Random House LLC.

Visit us on the Web! rhcbooks.com

Educators and librarians, for a variety of teaching tools, visit us at RHTeachersLibrarians.com

Library of Congress Cataloging-in-Publication Data is available upon request.
ISBN 978-0-593-42958-7 (hc) — ISBN 978-0-593-42960-0 (ebook)

The text of this book is set in 11.3-point Charlotte Std. Book.
Interior design by Cathy Bobak

Printed in the United States of America
10 9 8 7 6 5 4 3 2 1
First Edition

For Madison, Jake, and Jerry, and
friendships forged in fire.
And for Steve, who sparked the flame.

CHAPTER ONE

Deep in the Glades, as the sun set on the evening of the winter solstice, two girls crept toward a sleeping dragon-gator. One held a pair of tweezers; the other kept her hands buried deep in the pockets of her blue cotton dress. Both took quiet, careful steps through the marsh, the brackish water nearly up to their knees, and their skirts tied to keep them from getting ruined.

"I don't want to do this," Larkin, the girl with the tweezers, whispered. Her blond hair hung in two stick-straight braids, each tied with a scrap of yellow ribbon. A few strands had slipped free, shoved hastily behind her ears.

"But you want the scale," the other girl, Cordelia, whispered back. She was taller by a couple of inches, with hair the color of mahogany bark. It desperately needed brushing, but that suited her. Everything about Cordelia was a bit untamed. Even the sky-blue dress she wore—the best one she owned—was hopelessly wrinkled.

Larkin didn't *want* the scale. She *needed* the scale. But there was no time to explain that when they were already running late, and even if there were, she wasn't sure Cordelia would understand the difference between *wanting* and *needing*. Larkin didn't think Cordelia knew what it was to need something, only to have everything.

She pushed the flare of jealousy from her mind and focused on the sleeping dragon-gator. "Can't you do it?" she asked her friend, but Cordelia shook her head.

"It has to be you. And don't be so dramatic—it's just a dragon-gator," Cordelia said, though she was careful to keep her voice low to avoid drawing its attention.

"A dragon-gator with sharp teeth and claws and a mouth big enough to swallow me whole," Larkin muttered under her breath even as she took a step closer, then another, Cordelia at her side.

"A *sleeping* dragon-gator whose big mouth isn't good for anything more than snoring," Cordelia countered. "Besides, they're docile. You know that."

Larkin did know that. She knew it the same way she knew that the phoenix-flies that illuminated the banyan trees always flickered back to life eventually or that marsh-maids swimming in the Beguilement River were more illusion than flesh and bone—no matter how many times she told herself those things were true, it was difficult to remember when she came face to face with the creatures in question.

Especially when the face of said creature was so big and scaly and full of teeth.

"Don't be such a baby," Cordelia whispered, nudging Larkin forward.

Larkin shot Cordelia a glare before turning her gaze back to the creature sprawled out on the log, its talons hanging down on either side, skimming the water, its eyes closed. Avocado-green wings draped down over its back like a blanket. It was so still that it could have been carved from moss-covered stone, if not for the ever so slight flare of its nostrils and the steady rise and fall of its chest.

She glanced back at Cordelia, hoping her friend would stop her, but instead, Cordelia's dark brown eyes met hers like a dare and Larkin heard her words echo through her mind. *Don't be such a baby.*

Larkin *wasn't* a baby. She was eleven—only a few months younger than Cordelia, who had just turned twelve, though sometimes that small distance felt like eons. They were the same age, more or less, but Cordelia always seemed so much older and wiser, and Larkin always felt like . . . well, like a baby in comparison. But she was determined to prove Cordelia and herself wrong. Squaring her shoulders, she took a step closer to the dragon-gator, then another, all the while watching the steady rise and fall of its chest. The sun was just dipping below the horizon, which meant she and Cordelia were officially late for the solstice party.

Part of her wanted to leave now, walk away from the dragon-gator and run to the party before they missed all the best treats, but they couldn't go without that scale. Larkin would rather miss the party altogether—not to mention the fact that Cordelia would call her a coward in that scathing voice that could strip the leaves off a mangrove, and that might be even worse. In fact, Larkin decided, a dragon-gator bite might even be preferable.

When she was within arm's reach of the creature, Larkin readied the tweezers she'd stolen from her mother's vanity, holding them the way she'd seen her mother do when she plucked errant hairs from her eyebrows.

She slid her eyes over the dragon-gator's broad back, looking for the perfect scale, big but not too big, bright but not too bright, and soft enough that it would come away with ease. She found just such a scale in the space between the dragon-gator's wings—roughly the size of her thumbnail and the color of saw grass in sunlight.

With a shaking hand, Larkin reached toward the scale with the tweezers and pinched the edge of it firmly. Then, with all her might, she pulled.

The scale came loose; Cordelia gave a sharp inhale behind her, and Larkin went utterly still as the dragon-gator slowly blinked open its eyes, turning its golden gaze onto

Larkin. Its long tail snapped, hitting the back of her legs with a sharp sting.

"Ow!" Larkin exclaimed, rubbing the spot with her free hand.

In response, the dragon-gator lifted its head and let out a low growl that raised goose bumps on Larkin's arms.

It was a warning growl, telling Larkin to run. She *knew* she should run—but her feet wouldn't move. She felt frozen in place, unable to do more than stare openmouthed at the dragon-gator until a blur of pink sailed over her shoulder.

With a jerk of its head, the dragon-gator caught the pink thing between its jaws and began to chew, gooey strands stretching between its razor-sharp teeth. Taffy, Larkin realized, when she caught a hint of the dragon-gator's strawberry-scented breath. It watched them both as it chewed, its yellow eyes darting between Larkin and Cordelia, as if measuring them up and trying to decide if they were worth the effort of a chase. Then the dragon-gator laid its head on the log once more and went back to sleep.

"You owe me a piece of taffy," Cordelia said, calm as a summer breeze across the water.

Larkin turned to look at her friend, her heart still hammering so loud in her chest she was surprised the sound of it didn't wake the dragon-gator again. Cordelia's arms were crossed over her chest and she wore a smug smile.

"And a thank-you," Cordelia added.

Larkin let out a deep breath and shook her head, though the fear she'd felt staring the dragon-gator in the eyes hadn't left her yet—probably wouldn't leave her for some time. She tucked the tweezers and the scale into her dress pocket and walked toward Cordelia, trying to hide how her legs were shaking.

"Thank you," she said, matching Cordelia's calm voice. "And there will be cake at the solstice party. I'll get you a piece there—that should make for an even trade."

"It is *not* an even trade. The cake is *free*," Cordelia replied, but she linked her arm with Larkin's as both girls started back the way they came.

"You stole that taffy from your brother," Larkin countered.

"Exactly," Cordelia said, nodding. "I worked very hard for it."

"Would it have killed you to throw it *before* it hit me with its tail? That really hurt!"

"Less than its teeth would have," Cordelia pointed out.

And Larkin couldn't argue with that. Besides, she'd made it through with all her limbs, a lucky dragon-gator's scale in her pocket, and her best friend at her side. A stung leg was not much to complain about at all.

"Come on," Cordelia said, tugging Larkin along with her. "We're going to be late."

CHAPTER TWO

The party was well under way by the time Cordelia and Larkin made their way to the Labyrinth Tree. Music spilled through the air from the band set up in the corner, bright and loud and quick, underscored by the steady hum of conversation and laughter. There were people everywhere, dressed in their finest clothes—which, in the Glades, where most people worked outdoors, meant whatever they had with the fewest salt stains and patches.

There were many banyan trees in the Glades, but the Labyrinth Tree was the oldest of them all. It was hard to imagine that it had once been a sapling with a single slender trunk—its heart trunk—but that must have been the case ages ago, before the girls' parents, or even *their* parents, had ever taken their first breaths. Unlike most kinds of trees, banyans didn't only grow taller and thicker with time; they actually expanded, like the web of a spider.

True to its name, the Labyrinth Tree was a maze of trunks and branches, and it never seemed to look the same from one day to the next. It stretched out for acres in any direction and a person could very easily find themselves lost in it—Cordelia certainly had plenty of times. It was also the location of the Glades solstice parties. In the summer, that meant chargrilled mangoes topped with vanilla cream, sweet iced teas, and swimming in the nearby river. But the winter solstice party was their chance to break out hot cider spiced with cinnamon sticks, and bowls of warm stew, while everyone from the village came together to talk and dance and celebrate another season passing.

"You two are late," Larkin's mother, Minerva, said, sweeping toward them as they headed toward the cider table, her long violet dress fluttering behind her like a pair of dormant wings. Despite the accusation in her words, her mouth was curved into a wry smile.

"Sorry, Mom," Larkin said, her hand going to her pocket, where Cordelia knew the dragon-gator scale was tucked away. "We had to stop for something on the way."

Aunt Minerva raised a single eyebrow. "Will you tell me what it was?" she asked.

Larkin smiled slightly. "If it works, you'll be the first to know," she said. Cordelia understood why Larkin was being vague. She'd seen the disappointment and embarrassment on Larkin's face every time she'd tried to use magic and failed.

Larkin was the daughter of the Witch of the Glades, and she was eleven years old now, but still she hadn't managed to light a candle or change her hair color or even levitate a feather—all things the magic books in Aunt Minerva's library said that witches Larkin's age were supposed to be able to do. And ever since Larkin's younger brother, Zephyr, had gotten his powers at only nine, Larkin had become even more desperate to discover her own.

"Where's Zephyr?" Cordelia asked, looking around for him or for her own brother, Dash. Where one was, the other was never too far away.

"I saw him and Dash half an hour ago, but not since then," Aunt Minerva said, a small frown creasing her forehead, her eyes on the small group of children about Zephyr and Dash's age playing around a cluster of the Labyrinth Tree's trunks. Cordelia recognized them from Zephyr and Dash's class, kids they'd played with after school; a few of them had even come over for dinner and sleepovers. But there was no sign of either boy there now.

"We'll find them," Cordelia said.

Aunt Minerva lifted her shoulder in a casual shrug. "Hopefully, before they find a way to burn everything to the ground, hmm?" she said.

Cordelia thought she was only half joking. At the summer solstice party, Zephyr and Dash got into the fireworks that had been ordered all the way from the northern cities and had managed to blow a hole the size of a watermelon through a tree. No one was hurt and the fire had been contained quickly, but it had done quite a bit of damage. And that was *before* Zephyr had come into his magic. Who knew what trouble those two could make now?

Someone called Aunt Minerva's name, and after giving both girls a quick squeeze on the shoulder, Aunt Minerva melted back into the crowd, leaving Cordelia and Larkin alone to mingle with the other partygoers. They passed by a table of drinks, and both girls picked up mugs of hot apple cider with cinnamon sticks floating on top.

"When are you going to try it?" Cordelia asked, blowing on her cider to cool it, sending ripples across the amber surface.

Cordelia didn't specify what she meant, but she didn't have to. Larkin's free hand went back to rest on the pocket where she kept the dragon-gator scale.

"Later," she said, shaking her head. "Mom always says to eat a good meal first."

"I figured she said that to make you eat your veggies," Cordelia said, giving Larkin a shrewd look. "You sure you're not procrastinating?"

"Of course not," Larkin said, but Cordelia knew she was lying. When she fixed Larkin with a knowing look, Larkin rolled her eyes. "I'll do it tonight," she said, before changing the subject.

Cordelia opened her mouth to speak, but before she could say another word, something small and hard hit her on the back of the neck.

"Ow!" Cordelia said with a scowl, clapping a hand over the spot and catching the offending projectile—a peanut. "What the bog?"

Cordelia swung her gaze around, searching the tree branches above until her eyes lit on two small, shadowy figures snickering in the branches high above the ground.

"Found Zephyr and Dash," Cordelia said to Larkin, nodding toward them.

"Sorry!" Dash called down, failing to sound completely apologetic. "It was an accident!"

"We weren't aiming for you," Zephyr added, casting a meaningful glance a few feet away, where a tall, imposing woman wearing an elaborate updo stood, her mouth curved into a frown that looked to be carved in stone.

Cordelia and Larkin exchanged a glance before Cordelia grabbed a tree branch and pulled herself up, Larkin just a step behind her. It wasn't easy to climb in dresses, though Larkin had more practice at it than Cordelia, who usually preferred leggings and shorts, but in a few minutes, both girls found themselves comfortable perches just beside their brothers.

"Isn't that Tarquin's mom?" Cordelia asked, looking down at the frowning woman, who she remembered from when she accompanied her mother to get her hair cut at the salon. Tarquin had been friends with Zephyr and Dash since they were toddlers; Cordelia recalled seeing him tonight, playing with the other kids around the Labyrinth Tree.

Zephyr shrugged, but his expression was clouded. He was never very good at hiding his feelings, and Cordelia could read the hurt in his expression clearly in his red cheeks and clenched jaw.

"Tarquin isn't allowed to play with Zephyr anymore," Dash said quietly. He looked down at the cup of peanuts he held between his knees, reaching in to pick one up before dropping it. Unlike the last one, it fell right into Tarquin's mom's elaborate updo. From this vantage point, Larkin could count at least ten other peanuts embedded in her hair.

A small, hot flame of anger sparked in Cordelia's chest. "Because of . . . ?"

Cordelia didn't finish the question, but she didn't have to. Zephyr and Dash both nodded. Beside her, Larkin let out a long exhale.

Magic manifested in different ways for different people. Aunt Minerva told them that hers came when she was eleven years old, when she stood beneath the light of a full moon on the winter solstice and *felt* magic tingling in her fingers and toes and just knew that if she didn't use it, she would turn inside out. And so she had—she'd lifted her hands over her head and tilted her face toward the moon and let out an ear-piercing scream that shook the leaves off the trees around her and caused them to fall into flamingo-pink piles.

That had been Larkin's favorite story for as long as Cordelia could remember. She'd asked for it again and again when they were younger; and now, Cordelia would guess, Larkin knew it by heart. Cordelia liked it too—it had a certain mythos to it, and maybe even more important, she knew it gave Larkin hope. After all, Larkin herself was still eleven for a couple more months. She had time.

But then Zephyr had let out a great big sneeze in the middle of Cordelia's twelfth birthday party and melted her elaborately decorated cake to a puddle of rainbow-streaked goo with his boogers.

It did *not* have the same charm as Aunt Minerva's story—in fact, it had made Zephyr something of a pariah in the Glades. No matter how many times Aunt Minerva had assured everyone that Zephyr wasn't dangerous—that he was being trained, that his boogers could be used for many other positive magical purposes, and that, once he learned to control his power, it might not take the form of boogers at all—still, no one seemed to be able to forget the image of the cake melting. No one seemed to be able to stop wondering what damage Zephyr could unleash, by accident or even by choice.

Larkin told Cordelia that she wasn't jealous of her brother. How could she be? She knew Zephyr was suffering, that he was afraid of himself. There was nothing to be envied in that. But Cordelia knew that Larkin hadn't been telling the whole truth.

Now, Cordelia held her hand up toward Dash, her own jaw tight with anger. "Give me one," she said.

Dash took a peanut out of his cup and passed it to Larkin, who looked below at Tarquin's mother. She took aim and threw it, watching it sail through the air and land in the woman's elegantly styled hair.

"Yes!" she said, pumping her fist in the air.

"I want to try," Cordelia said.

And so it continued, each of the four taking their turn to throw peanuts into the woman's hair, until Dash's throw went slightly wide, landing instead in her glass of champagne with a splash.

Tarquin's mother screamed in shock, her head swinging around and her cold eyes finding the four children sitting in the tree. Her eyebrows slanted down in a glare before she stalked off into the crowd.

"Oops," Dash said, though he was fighting a grin.

The grin faded quickly when the crowd parted again, this time making way for Cordelia and Dash's father, Oziris.

Looking around at the crowd of hundreds gathered tonight, it was hard to imagine that only twenty years before, there had been no one at all in the Glades—no one until

Cordelia's father had come, traveling where no one else had dared to travel in the southern swampy wilderness. He'd made a home here, and others had followed, because her father was the sort of man people followed. And now, two decades later, the Glades was a thriving village of more than five hundred people, with new arrivals coming from the north every season and Oziris as its leader.

Now he approached the base of the tree Larkin, Cordelia, Dash, and Zephyr had climbed and leaned against it, bracing himself on his elbows and peering up at them with a wry smile.

"I heard there were heathen children causing a ruckus and assumed they must be mine," he said.

Larkin and Zephyr had always called him Uncle Oziris, even though there was no blood shared between them. Sometimes, though, even that didn't seem like quite enough. It felt like their two families were mushed together, impossible to untangle, like the eight of them were a single unit— four children with four parents. It was natural, in a sense, for Oziris to claim all four as his.

"It was a joke," Dash told his dad, grinning.

"I doubt Allaria thought it was funny," he said. Allaria was Tarquin's mother.

"Well, we didn't think it was funny when she forbade Tarquin from playing with Zephyr," Larkin told him.

Oziris's eyes found hers and softened before shifting to Zephyr.

"Is that true, Zeph?" he asked.

Zephyr nodded. "No one's allowed to play with me anymore," he said. "And Tarquin's mom is trying to make me leave school. She says I'm a danger to the other kids."

Cordelia stiffened. She didn't know *that* part. Her father, however, didn't look surprised, merely tired.

"We aren't going to let her do that," he told Zephyr solemnly before looking at all four children. Cordelia wanted to believe him, but even the leader of the Glades had his limits, and this just might prove to be one of them. "Allaria is demanding an apology from you all."

"I'm *not* apologizing," Cordelia said.

"Me either," Larkin said.

"*She* should apologize," Dash added.

Zephyr stayed quiet, but nodded along.

Cordelia's father let out a long exhale, looking at each of them in turn. "It was a harmless prank," he said finally, mostly to himself. "I'll deal with her. You four make yourselves scarce, all right? And do try to keep the trouble to a minimum."

They nodded quickly and Oziris turned to leave before pausing.

"You're a good kid, Zeph," he said. "You're kind and considerate and brave and I know things have been hard, but your power doesn't define you. You're still you and that's what counts."

Zephyr looked like he didn't believe Oziris, but he nodded anyways and Oziris disappeared back into the crowd. Just as he did, the music coming from the band grew louder and the adults began to move to the dance-floor section of the party, pairing off. Cordelia caught sight of her father reaching her mother and taking her hand, leading her onto the dance floor as well. Cordelia wrinkled her nose and turned away. She knew her parents were in love, but she didn't want to have to see them act like it.

"Ewww," Dash said, apparently seeing the same thing.

"Let's get out of here before *we* have to dance," Zephyr said, and he and Dash scurried off, away from the dance floor.

"Remember to stay out of trouble!" Larkin called after them.

Amidst the dancing, Cordelia noticed a group of boys from her and Larkin's class—Atticus, Basil, and Wynn—looking at them from across the dance floor. They took turns nudging one another and mumbling, nodding toward her and Larkin.

Larkin noticed too. "Are they . . . daring each other to ask us to dance?" she asked.

"Looks that way," Cordelia said, frowning. She thought that if Atticus asked her to dance on his own, she might say yes, but she didn't want to be his dare.

She glanced at the sky above, where the full moon was

beginning to peek out from the clusters of fluffy moonlit clouds.

"It's time," she said. Larkin followed her gaze, and her skin turned a shade paler. After a second, though, she nodded.

"It's time," she repeated.

CHAPTER THREE

Everything was exactly as it should be—Larkin had made sure of it. Her magic hadn't manifested on its own, so she had to help it along. If that meant re-creating the exact circumstances of her mother's story, so be it. And so tonight was the night: the winter solstice, when the moon was full. Tonight was the night she would claim her magic, she was sure of it. She even had the dragon-gator scale in her pocket, a talisman for good luck. Everything was exactly as it should be.

"Okay," Cordelia said over her shoulder, all business as they cut through the crowd, Cordelia leading the way as usual. "How do you want to do this, Lark?"

Every part of Larkin felt like it was buzzing. That was what her mother had said, wasn't it? That the first time she used magic, she felt it buzzing through her. It was happening! It *felt* like nerves, but maybe that was just what magic felt like.

"The clearing," Larkin said, her voice coming out steady and sure. "Where you can see the moon. That'll be the best spot."

She didn't know why she thought this. There was no evidence to support it, no stories about it, not even a gut feeling, really. But it was something she could control, so Larkin latched on to the thought. "Yes, the clearing," she said again. "Definitely."

Cordelia nodded as if this made perfect sense, and they wound through the crowd until they found it. The trees were strung with phoenix-fly lights and there were two large banquet tables, one set with glasses of wine and strawberry juice, the other set with a feast of fileted fish, fried frog legs, roasted carrots, and orange tarts. A crowd was there as well, but there was no canopy of tree branches overhead. Instead, the evening sky shone down, dotted with stars that were just beginning to wink their way into sight and dominated by the full moon.

Larkin thought about suggesting a more secluded spot, away from witnesses in case she failed again, but she quickly pushed the idea aside. She *wasn't* going to fail. She was going to do magic and she *wanted* everyone to see it, to show all of the Glades exactly what she was capable of.

"Are you ready?" Cordelia asked.

No, Larkin wanted to say. *No, I'm not ready at all. I'll never be ready. My magic will never come. I'll always be thoroughly ordinary, not smart enough or funny enough or brave enough.*

But the prospect of that terrified Larkin more than the prospect of failing yet again. She wouldn't fail this time, she told herself. She couldn't fail this time. Not on the winter solstice, with the full moon overhead and the dragon-gator scale in her pocket. Failure wasn't possible. She was her mother's daughter and tonight was the night she was going to claim her birthright. She knew it deep in her bones and she wouldn't let herself consider the alternative.

"I'm ready," she told Cordelia because she simply *had to be ready,* whether she felt it or not.

"Okay, then," Cordelia said, grinning. "Do it."

Larkin closed her eyes, focusing on the nerves buzzing through her—the *magic* buzzing through her, she corrected. She thought about what happened next in her mother's story, how she said she felt like she had to unleash the magic inside her. Well, Larkin certainly felt *that,* even if it wasn't in the way she'd imagined it. Then her mother said she had let out an ear-piercing scream. So scream is exactly what Larkin did. She opened her mouth and screamed as loud as she could. So loud that the flocks of egrets and herons and kingfishers that were gathered in the Labyrinth Tree's branches took flight, letting out indignant cries as they did. So loud that Cordelia got goose bumps on her arms. So

21

loud that several of the adults around them dropped their glasses, causing them to shatter against the rocky ground.

When Larkin's scream finally died off, the whole of the Glades seemed to hold its breath. No one spoke, no one moved, even the wind itself seemed to stop blowing.

Nothing happened. Nothing at all.

And then the Glades exhaled and life resumed as it had been before, with no magic, no whisper of enchantment. Just bewildered conversation and looks directed at Larkin. There were some scowls, some concern, but everyone seemed to quickly decide it was just one of the heathen witch's heathen children, acting up and making a scene. No one paid Larkin any more mind.

No one except her mother, who stood at the center of the crowd and yet apart from it, watching Larkin with understanding and pity in her eyes.

It was the pity that was too much to bear. Larkin felt her throat grow tight, all the dashed hope and loss and desperation finally breaking within her. Tears came hot and quick and when her mother took a step toward her, Larkin turned and ran, Cordelia trailing behind, in her wake for once.

CHAPTER FOUR

Larkin ran away from the party and Cordelia followed her, the two of them heading deeper into the tangle of the Labyrinth Tree. Cordelia didn't know what to say as she trailed after her friend. After a few minutes, Larkin stopped short, out of breath, doubling over and bracing her hands on her knees. She didn't look up, but the shaking of her shoulders told Larkin that she was crying. Cordelia set a gentle hand on her friend's back—words still failed her, but she wanted to do *something* to make Larkin feel better.

Larkin straightened up, wiping her eyes with her hand and giving one last sniffle. A phoenix-fly danced near her face, its light glowing soft and golden before it fell to the ground beside her with a mournful buzz, its light flickering out—dramatic, as phoenix-flies always were in their temporary deaths. Sure enough, a few heartbeats later, the phoenix-fly's light revived and it took to the air once more, flitting just in front of Cordelia's face before disappearing back into the shelter of the Labyrinth Tree.

Normally, Larkin liked to watch the phoenix-flies go through their cycle of life and death—she said it was poetic, though Cordelia had never had much patience for the spectacle, poetic or not. But now, Larkin didn't even blink.

"We'll try again," Cordelia told her when the silence grew to be too much.

Larkin laughed, but it sounded sad. "So I can embarrass myself again?" she asked. "I know what they must think of me. The powerless daughter of Minerva of the Glades, with all the weirdness but none of the magic."

Cordelia opened her mouth to tell her that wasn't true but quickly closed it again. No one would have dared say anything like that to Cordelia, but that didn't mean they didn't say it to each other. The people of the Glades needed the magic Larkin's mother provided—the potions that kept them healthy, the charms that made their crops grow and businesses thrive, the enchantments that made their lives just a bit easier. Cordelia's father had said plenty of times that while he'd been the first one to settle in the Glades, it never would have flourished without Aunt Minerva and her magic. But her father also said that people had a tendency to fear what they didn't understand, and since no one truly understood magic, the village was also a little bit afraid of Aunt Minerva, and her family too.

Which, to Cordelia, seemed ridiculous. There was nothing frightening about Aunt Minerva. Even when Cordelia, Larkin, and their brothers had been playing tag in the house and Cordelia knocked over a vase, shattering it, Minerva hadn't even raised her voice, much less cast some sort of spell. She'd just asked Cordelia to clean up the mess, before sending them all outside to play.

"You're not weird," Cordelia told Larkin instead. "Not weirder than anyone else, at least."

A smile flickered across Larkin's face, but it was gone quicker than a phoenix-fly's flash.

"What if my magic never comes?" she asked after a moment. "I'm not good at anything, Cor—not like you. You're better at school, and sports, and everything else—"

"I'm not—" Cordelia started to say, but Larkin interrupted.

"You *are*," she insisted, and Cordelia felt the sharp edge of her voice like broken glass. "Like the other day in music class, when Mr. Dolovan started teaching us how to play panpipes. You were the best in class and you didn't even have to try! You're good at everything, so you can do whatever you want when you grow up. I'm not good at anything like that."

Again, Cordelia was stunned speechless. She *had* taken to playing panpipes easier than the other kids in their class.

And she did regularly get top marks on tests and essays. Every time her parents came back from a meeting with her teachers, they glowed with pride, saying she excelled in all her lessons.

But Cordelia didn't love anything as much as Larkin loved magic—even if it didn't love her back. There were times when Cordelia wondered what would happen if Larkin's magic came—would she spend all her time in lessons? Would she have time to play still? Would she have time for Cordelia at all? The thought was an ugly thing, worming into her head and refusing to leave. She and Larkin had always shared everything—toys, hobbies, even families, it seemed. Magic, though, they couldn't share. That would be for Larkin alone, and so there was a small part of Cordelia that was relieved every time Larkin's magic failed. There was a part of her that hoped it never came.

Cordelia couldn't tell Larkin any of that. Instead, she reached out to put an arm around Larkin's shoulders and let Larkin rest her head on her shoulder.

"You're good at plenty of things," Cordelia assured her. "Even if your magic never shows up, Lark, you'll be fine. We'll be fine. We've got each other."

Cordelia hoped the words would be reassuring, but Larkin didn't seem reassured. Instead, she straightened up, pulling away from Cordelia and crossing her arms over her chest.

"I don't want to go back to the party," she said. "I can't stand everyone looking at me."

"The party was boring anyways," Cordelia told her, even though she desperately wanted to go back and get one of those mango tarts. "Let's just stay here."

CHAPTER FIVE

Larkin and Zephyr ended up staying over at Cordelia and Dash's after the winter solstice party wound to a close later that night. It was well past their bedtime and all four of them fell asleep as soon as they climbed into their beds.

It felt like mere moments later that Cordelia awoke to a gentle hand on her shoulder. She blinked her eyes open, letting them adjust to her pitch-dark bedroom. She could make out Larkin sitting up in the narrow bed that pulled out from beneath hers for sleepovers, looking just as bewildered as she felt and, beyond her, Dash and Zephyr standing in the doorway in their pajamas, each with a blanket hanging over their shoulders like a cape. And there, standing above Cordelia with his hand on her shoulder, was her dad.

"It's the middle of the night," she croaked out, rolling away from him and burying her face in the pillow.

"I know, I know," her dad said, his soft, deep voice barely reaching her through the pillow's defense. "But I want to show you something. I promise it will be worth it."

Cordelia groaned and rolled back over to look at her dad. A big part of her wanted to tell him to go away, that whatever he wanted to show her couldn't possibly be as interesting to her as sleep was. But something stopped her. Curiosity maybe. After all, her dad didn't make promises lightly, and since Larkin was already climbing out of her bed and crossing the room to join their brothers, Cordelia didn't want to be the only one who missed out. She let out a dramatic sigh and pushed off her covers with a little more force than necessary.

"And here I thought I had another year or so before you turned into a terrible teenager," her dad commented, passing her and Larkin their own blankets. Even though the Glades never got as cold as the adults said the North got, it did get a little chilly in the winter at night.

Cordelia pulled the blanket close around her and rolled her eyes. "I just want my sleep," she told him.

"Spoken like a true terrible teenager," he said, nodding somberly. "Next thing I know, you'll be slamming doors and going on dates and telling me I just don't understand what you're going through."

Nothing about being a teenager sounded like fun to Cordelia, but she wasn't about to tell her dad that. "Maybe

I'll practice the door slamming now," she told him instead. "Just to make sure I understand how it works."

Her dad laughed, placing a hand on her back to usher her toward the others. "Just don't grow up too fast, Cor," he told her before looking at the others. "Ready for the surprise?"

The four children exchanged bewildered looks, but this wasn't the first time Oziris had led them on some kind of adventure. They had never regretted following him before. So they did the only thing they could—they nodded and let him lead them out of the room and down the winding hall.

Blankets drawn tight around their shoulders, the four of them followed him up the stairs, then up another set that led to the house's flat roof.

The kids had been on the roof plenty of times—just the week before, Cordelia's mom had brought them up to have a picnic lunch in the sun—but they'd never seen it at night-time. The house was tall enough that the roof stood higher than the tops of the trees, letting the night sky take up the entire view above. When Cordelia tilted her head back, all she could see was ink-black sky, the bright full moon, and more stars than she could count in a lifetime.

And then . . . *oh*.

"Did you see it?" her dad asked, looking down at her, but Cordelia kept her gaze focused on the sky.

"A star fell," she said, feeling like all the breath had left her lungs. "It was there, and then it fell and disappeared."

"No way," Dash said, peering up as well. Zephyr and Larkin quickly followed suit, their own eyes scanning the sky. They all watched as another star streaked across, then another.

"It's not just the winter solstice tonight, not just a full moon . . . it's also a star shower. A night like this might not come again in our lifetimes," her dad said. "I wanted you all to see it."

The four of them spread out their blankets on the rooftop, side by side, and lay down, staring up at the sky and watching the stars fall.

"Where do they go?" Zephyr asked after a moment of awed silence.

Oziris didn't answer at first. "I don't know," he said finally. "I don't know where they come from either, but I like to think it's the same place. What I *do* know is that you can make wishes on them."

Cordelia glanced at her dad, raising a skeptical eyebrow. "Wishes?" she asked. "Like with birthday candles? I asked for a pony six years in a row and I never got one."

He laughed, shaking his head. "Candles and stars are different. There's real magic in stars—everyone knows that."

At the mention of magic, Cordelia cut her eyes toward Larkin, who had been mostly quiet ever since they'd left the Labyrinth Tree. Her friend's face was tilted up toward the sky now, but she could see the almost imperceptible flinch.

"No one needs magic," Cordelia told her dad sharply. "It's overrated and more trouble than it's worth—just ask Zeph."

Zephyr looked at her, surprised to be mentioned, but after a second, he nodded slowly. "It is a lot of trouble," he agreed.

Oziris let out a long sigh. "Magic is everywhere," he said after a moment. "It's in the stars, yes, and it's in Zephyr's boogers"—that caused Dash and Zephyr to burst out in laughter—"but it's in you and me as well. It's in the swamp, in the water and the trees and all the creatures who call it home. Magic is in the air. It's in all of us."

"It's not in me," Larkin said, so quietly that Cordelia could barely hear her, even though only a few inches separated them. Oziris heard her, though. He offered Larkin a reassuring smile that Larkin didn't quite manage to return.

"Did I ever tell you all about the marsh-maid who couldn't sing?" he asked.

Cordelia and the others shook their heads. Oziris had told them countless stories, but she didn't think that had been one of them.

"Well," Oziris said, his voice shifting ever so slightly into what Cordelia thought of as his Story Voice—a little deeper and more melodic than how he usually spoke. "Once, there was a marsh-maid who couldn't sing. Every time she opened her mouth, no sound came out at all. Now, you know marsh-maids love singing more than anything, so many of the other marsh-maids were cruel to her. They wouldn't play with her or swim near her and they called her awful names."

"What kind of names?" Dash asked.

"Names that don't translate well to any human tongues, I'm afraid," Oziris said, reaching out to ruffle Dash's hair. "But you can use your imagination." When Dash's smile turned devious, Oziris laughed. "As long as they don't include any of those words your mother's forbidden you from saying." Dash's smile turned into a pout.

"But as I was saying," Oziris continued, "the marsh-maid was mocked and teased and lonely because no one wanted to be friends with a marsh-maid who couldn't sing. And she was very sad because she felt useless—after all, what is the point of a marsh-maid who can't sing?"

Next to Cordelia, Larkin burrowed farther beneath the blanket, so only her face was visible above it. She was frowning up at the stars, but Cordelia knew she was hanging on Oziris's every word.

"One day, the other marsh-maids were lounging in the shallow part of the river, singing in the light of the afternoon sun, while the voiceless marsh-maid watched from the shadows, desperately wishing she could join them; still, whenever she opened her mouth to sing, only silence came out. But their song dug beneath her skin and all the sadness and loneliness and anger she'd been keeping to herself bubbled to the surface and she couldn't restrain herself anymore."

"She finally sang?" Larkin asked quietly.

Oziris smiled at her. "No, Larkin. She began to dance. In the shadows of the mangroves at first, but soon she came out into the sun, where the other marsh-maids could see her. They sang, she danced, and the song was all the more beautiful because of it. From that day forward, the marsh-maid felt at home with her pod."

"Even though they'd made fun of her?" Zephyr asked, frowning.

"Well, marsh-maids are a lot like people in some ways— they make mistakes. They apologized and made amends, and in time, the dancing marsh-maid forgave them. And from that day forward, whenever the marsh-maids sang, she danced, and together they made beautiful music."

After Oziris finished the story, Larkin didn't say anything for a moment. "She was lucky she could dance, though," she said after a moment. "Some of us aren't good at anything."

"You're good at plenty of things," Oziris told her. "Besides, your magic could still appear, even if it isn't in the way you expect."

"And if it doesn't?" Larkin asked.

"Everyone has magic in them, Lark. Just because it doesn't rise to the surface doesn't mean it isn't there, inside you. Like the marsh-maid's song—she couldn't sing it, but she could dance it. I don't have any kind of powers. Neither does Aunt Thalia. Cordelia and Dash likely never will either. Do you think any of us are any lesser because of that?" he asked.

"Of course not!" Larkin said, bolting upright.

Oziris smiled gently. "Then why would it make you any lesser?" he asked her.

Larkin opened her mouth and closed it again several times, but no words came out.

"Sometimes," Oziris continued, "it's a lot easier to be kind to others than it is to be kind to ourselves. But kindness is its own kind of magic. And it's the kind of magic you can choose."

Larkin bit her lip, her shoulders slumping, but after a second, she lay back down, turning her attention again to the sky and the stars now streaking across it at a constant pace.

"Ready to make some wishes?" Oziris asked. "Remember— you can't say them out loud."

Cordelia closed her eyes for a moment, shutting out the stars altogether, before opening them again. She wasn't sure if she believed in wishes—no matter what her dad said, wishing on anything seemed babyish. But in that moment, staring up at an impossibly wide sky, surrounded by people who loved her, Cordelia felt both small and large, insignificant and vital. She felt like anything was possible, like anything could happen. The idea terrified her.

Her eyes tracked a star, watching it fall in a blur of blinding white.

I wish everything could stay exactly like this, always.

It was, she realized when her eyes grew heavy with sleep and her mind turned fuzzy at the edges, perhaps the only truly impossible wish.

CHAPTER SIX

When Cordelia opened her eyes again, she found herself back in her bed, the covers tucked snugly around her and the sky outside her window only just beginning to lighten. It was still hours before she usually woke up on the weekend, and sleepiness made her limbs feel heavy and soft, but she knew she wouldn't be falling back asleep.

A gnawing sense of dread had made itself at home in the pit of her stomach. Every time she closed her eyes, she thought about what Larkin had said the day before: *"You're good at everything."*

She knew Larkin meant it as a compliment, but all Cordelia could think was that, of all those things she was good at, she didn't *love* any of them—not playing panpipes or math or writing or dancing. Not the way Larkin loved magic.

Cordelia looked out her window, at the pinkening dawn sky. Her father was always up with the sun—she could talk to him about how she was feeling. After all, her father always gave the best advice. Without another thought, Cordelia slipped out of bed and carefully climbed over Larkin's sleeping form on the trundle bed below.

As soon as she opened the door, she knew something was wrong.

Aunt Minerva was standing outside the door to Cordelia's parents' bedroom, speaking with Dr. Lavinia in hushed voices that Cordelia couldn't hear. For a moment, she could only stare at them, her brain still half-asleep and struggling to make sense of what both of them were doing here, in her house, at dawn.

"Cordelia."

Cordelia spun toward the sound of her name to find her mother standing in the kitchen doorway holding a mug of coffee. Her hands were shaking ever so slightly, Cordelia noticed, and when she looked closer, she realized her mother had been crying.

Everyone in the Glades referred to her mother as the ice queen behind her back—Cordelia had heard them more than a few times and it had always sparked her anger, even if she only knew of ice the same way she knew of snow, through stories. Cordelia knew her mother wasn't cold; she'd felt the warmth of her smile, felt the comfort of her arms wrapping around her, heard the joy in her laugh. She'd seen how her mother came alive in her pottery studio, molding pots and bowls and all manner of other things, never afraid to get her hands dirty. But her mother kept her emotions close to her, hidden beneath her skin most of the time.

Cordelia realized she had never, ever seen her mother cry.

"What's wrong?" Cordelia asked her before glancing back at Aunt Minerva and Dr. Lavinia, both of whom were staring at her now. Aunt Minerva looked like she'd been crying too, and even Dr. Lavinia, usually smiling and happy, looked deeply troubled.

Her mother's hand came down on her shoulder and she led her down the hall and through the kitchen doors, but she didn't answer Cordelia's question. So Cordelia asked two more.

"What are they doing here?" she asked. "Is Dad sick?"

Her mother shook her head, opening her mouth to speak before closing it again. "Come sit," she said, urging Cordelia into a chair at the breakfast table. Part of Cordelia wanted to jump to her feet, to demand an answer, but suddenly she was terrified of what that answer might be, so she stayed sitting.

The door to the kitchen opened and Aunt Minerva came in, though there was no sign or Dr. Lavinia. When she looked at Cordelia, her eyes were full of pity, and the sight of it turned Cordelia's stomach.

"Where's Dad?" she asked, looking between them. "I want to see Dad."

"Cordelia—" her mother began.

"Fine," she said, getting to her feet. "I'll get him. Is he still in bed?"

She started for the door, but Aunt Minerva stepped in front of it, blocking her way.

"Cordelia—" she said, her voice soft, but Cordelia wouldn't—*couldn't*—hear what she was going to say next.

She tried to push past her, but Aunt Minerva held her ground, blocking the door. Her mother grabbed hold of her shoulder and in the space of a breath, her mother had her arms around her, holding Cordelia tight.

"He didn't wake up this morning, Cor," her mother said, her voice breaking. "I don't know . . . I can't . . . he just didn't wake up."

"He's still asleep?" Cordelia asked, her voice muffled against her mother's shoulder.

Neither of them replied for a long moment. Cordelia's mother's shoulders began to shake and Cordelia realized she was sobbing.

"He died, Cordelia," Aunt Minerva said, her own voice breaking on that word. *Died.*

The word shattered something in Cordelia too, echoing through her mind. *Died. Died. Died.* She struggled to break free of her mother's embrace, but she couldn't.

She was dimly aware of both her mother and Aunt Minerva saying her name, of a cry that didn't feel entirely like hers, even though she felt it in her throat. And then she wasn't aware of anything, apart from that feeling of dread in her belly that had finally grown large enough to swallow her whole.

CHAPTER SEVEN

Unmoorings were a ceremony for the living who mourned, not the dead they honored. That was what Cordelia had always heard said. But in the three days since her father had become the latter, Cordelia had felt stuck somewhere in between, like a part of her had died with him. She knew that wasn't true, and if her mother were her usual self, she would have called her melodramatic for even thinking it. But Cordelia suspected her mother felt stuck as well.

Most days, her mother slept until noon, leaving Cordelia and Dash to fend for themselves, though Larkin, Zephyr, and their parents were always over by the time breakfast was done. When her mother was awake, she almost seemed to be sleepwalking through the day, until it was bedtime once again. Cordelia and Dash had both been falling asleep in bed with her, something Cordelia hadn't done in years.

Whatever the case might have been, the unmooring for her father didn't feel particularly for Cordelia's benefit. It just felt silly: everyone standing together as the sun dipped below the horizon, the handmade paper boats and the small candles they held, the letters people wrote—as if her father would ever be able to read them.

At the last unmooring Cordelia had attended, for her grandmother three years before, she'd liked the ritual of it. She remembered standing on the shore, just like this, as the sun set on the marsh, holding a candle in her hands. She remembered the silence that stretched out, so quiet she could hear her father's deep breaths, and tried to match her own to them. She remembered the sound of the wind blowing through the saw grass, how it sounded like voices whispering into the evening.

"The voices of those we've lost," her father had told her.

Cordelia tried to listen, but she couldn't hear anything that sounded like words.

"What is she saying to you?" Cordelia asked.

Her father's eyes had stayed on the horizon, but he'd smiled softly. "It's not words, exactly," he said. "It's a feeling. She's telling me she's all right. She's telling me she loves me—loves you and your mom and your brother too—and she's telling me to be happy."

Cordelia liked the thought of getting a message from her grandmother, so she turned her gaze to the horizon as well and listened as hard as she could and she told herself she heard the same messages. That her grandmother was okay. That she loved her. That she wanted her to be happy.

Now Cordelia tried again. She listened with everything she had, desperate to hear her father's voice one more time, desperate to feel even the slightest whisper of his presence. But when the wind blew through the saw grass, all she heard was wind.

The entirety of the Glades had come out for the unmooring, hundreds of people stretching out across the shoreline with their little paper boats and candles in hand.

People will want to pay their respects, her mother had told her beforehand, so she knew what to expect. *Your father was very loved by many.*

Looking out at the crowd now, though, Cordelia realized she never understood just how many people there were who held a piece of her father in their hearts. There were people she recognized—Aunt Minerva and Zephyr and Larkin, her father's closest friends, the baker they visited every week, the carpenter who had fixed their roof after a hurricane a few months ago, Cordelia and Dash's friends from school and their parents. But there were so many others Cordelia didn't know. She knew that her father had founded the Glades, that he acted as its leader; she knew that people—even total strangers—knew him, but it was easy to forget about them. Usually, he was just her dad, the sun in a universe she shared only with her family.

A strange sensation took root in Cordelia's stomach. It took her a moment to recognize it for what it was—anger.

No, anger wasn't the right word for it. It burned through her blood, hot as lava, threatening to swallow her whole. *Fury.*

All these people with their boats and candles, with their handwritten letters and memories of her father to set off into the swamp—they didn't know him, not really. He wasn't theirs, he was *hers.* And now he was gone and none of these people could possibly understand how she felt, the size of the hole left behind in her heart. How dare they pretend they did?

She pulled away from her mother and brother and started away from the shore, back toward the line of cypress trees, alone. Her stiff black mourning dress suddenly felt too tight around her chest. She couldn't breathe.

"Cordelia!"

She was vaguely aware of her mother calling for her, but she ignored her. The crowd of people parted before her, though she almost wished someone would try to stop her. Just now, she would welcome the chance to scream at the top of her lungs, to hit and kick anyone who laid a hand on her. The fury in her had to go somewhere before it ate her alive.

Cordelia made it into the copse of cypress trees, away from all the prying stares and her mother's shouts. She leaned back against a tree and let the fresh air flood her lungs.

Deep breath in, deep breath out, her father would always tell her when her mind swam like this, when her heartbeat started going too quick, her thoughts spinning out of control. *Remember to breathe and everything else will fall into place.*

Her chest grew tighter, but she forced herself to breathe. *Deep breath in, deep breath out. Deep breath in, deep breath out.*

A twig snapped and Cordelia whirled toward it, ready to scream and fight and rail against whoever or whatever it was.

But it was only Larkin. Her yellow-blond hair hung down in two plaits on either side of her round, freckled face. Larkin didn't say anything for a moment, and Cordelia was grateful for the silence. Grateful that Larkin was there, quiet but present. Grateful that she wasn't alone. It became easier to breathe with her there.

Deep breath in, deep breath out.

"Come on," Cordelia said after a moment, when she found her voice again. "Let's get out of here."

Larkin frowned, glancing back over her shoulder to the shore, where hundreds of people were gathered to say their goodbyes. "But the unmooring," she said. "Don't you want to say goodbye?"

"Why?" Cordelia asked, lifting her chin. "It's not like he can hear me. He's dead. Unmoorings are for the living, and I'd rather be anywhere else."

Larkin looked at her for a moment, in that way she always did, like she could see straight through Cordelia and everyone around her. Cordelia knew that wasn't the magic Larkin wanted so desperately, but she thought it was its own kind of power, seeing people the way Larkin did.

"All right," she said finally, nodding once, decisively. "Lead the way."

CHAPTER EIGHT

Larkin followed Cordelia as she stalked away from the unmooring, through the cypress grove and across a rickety dock that led into the marsh.

In the three days since Oziris's death, she'd spent at least a few hours a day with Cordelia, but the days had passed in a fog for both of them. Larkin could see how much her friend was crumbling, even if Cordelia wrapped herself in her anger to hide it, and Larkin didn't know how to fix it. There was nothing she could say or do to make things better. They'd been friends their whole lives, even though everyone said they were as different as night and day. Larkin knew better than most people that Oziris had been the glue that held Cordelia's world together.

Now she was here, but not really. She moved through the world like a ghost, her eyes glassy and her steps uncertain.

Cordelia's steps had never been uncertain. She'd always moved with purpose. It was something Larkin envied about her. But now she couldn't shake the feeling she was walking beside a stranger.

When they reached the end of the dock, Cordelia slipped off her shiny black shoes and knotted her long black dress at her knees. It would still get dirty, Larkin knew, but Cordelia's eyes were focused and bright and, if she was being honest, a bit frightening, so Larkin bit her tongue and followed suit with her own shoes and dress.

"Where are we going?" she asked, but Cordelia shook her head.

"I just want to walk. You can come or not, I don't care," she said before stepping down from the end of the dock and into the swamp, the brackish water going just past her ankles.

She didn't wait for an answer, walking farther away. In the shade of the towering cypress trees, Cordelia didn't look like the intimidating, sometimes terrifying girl Larkin had known for as long as she could remember. She didn't look like Larkin's best friend, who had always been a little taller, a little stronger, a little braver. She looked small and afraid and when Cordelia glanced back over her shoulder, Larkin knew deep in the pit of her stomach that Cordelia *did* care if Larkin followed, that she didn't want to be alone.

So Larkin followed Cordelia, like she always did, though when they fell into step beside one another, the murky water just below their knees and the air humid and still, Larkin felt as if she was the one leading the way for once.

"Do you want to talk about it?" Larkin asked. It felt like a silly question as soon as it had left her mouth, but Larkin's mother always said that talking about things made them more bearable.

Cordelia let out an inhuman noise, something that sounded like a dragon-gator's snarl. "Talking about it isn't going to change anything, Lark."

"And storming away from the unmooring to trek through the swamp will?" Larkin asked before she could stop herself.

Cordelia crossed her arms over her chest, slogging toward a small island made up of mangrove trees, their roots slithering like snakes through the water, searching for sand to draw nutrients from and add to the island. That was how it would expand—some mangrove islands could be miles long, though this one was a baby, just big enough for Cordelia to climb onto, and Larkin beside her.

Larkin thought of one of the stories Oziris told them, about why mangroves were tricksters and why their snake-like roots were prone to slither out and trip you or tickle you as you walked by. The memory lodged in her throat and she blinked back tears.

"The unmooring was stupid," Cordelia said after a moment.

"I thought it was a nice unmooring," Larkin said, just for the sake of saying something.

Cordelia snorted. "There's no such thing as a *nice unmooring*," she said. "I didn't feel him there, surrounded by all of those people. I thought maybe coming out here . . ." She paused, taking a moment to find the right words. "He loved it out here. This was where he taught us to swim, do you remember?" Larkin nodded, but before she could speak, Cordelia continued. "I thought . . . I thought I would feel closer to him here than I did there."

"And do you?" Larkin asked.

For a moment, Cordelia didn't say anything, her eyes focused on the horizon, where the sun, now fully set, had left behind a sky painted in shades of coral, gold, and indigo. Soon it would be dark out and they'd have to return home, but not yet.

"No," Cordelia said finally, her voice small. "I don't feel him anywhere at all. He's just . . . gone."

Larkin reached for Cordelia's hand, and to her surprise, Cordelia let her take it, squeezing it tight in her own as silent tears slipped down her cheeks.

Cordelia opened her mouth to say something else, but what it was, Larkin never found out, because in the same moment, a mangrove tendril slithered around Cordelia's ankle.

Mangroves were known tricksters, yes, but they had

never been malicious. Not until that mangrove grabbed hold of Cordelia's ankle and yanked her beneath the water's surface in one swift, sharp motion.

Larkin tried to hold on to her hand, but it was wrenched from her grip. Cordelia barely had time to scream before her head was pulled underwater and all Larkin could see were bubbles.

Without thinking, Larkin launched herself after her friend, plunging into the brackish water. The marsh wasn't deep—only two and a half feet at its deepest point—but with the mangrove root holding Cordelia down, it might as well have been the deepest part of the sea. Larkin saw her friend thrash and struggle to reach the surface.

Larkin grabbed hold of the root where it wrapped around Cordelia's ankle, trying to pry it off with her fingers, but it was no use—its hold was too tight. She could just make out Cordelia's face through the murky water, her eyes wide and panicked and desperate.

Larkin's mind was a blur of panic and fear, but through that she heard Oziris's voice, telling them the story of the mangroves of the Glades.

The reason the mangroves are such tricksters, Oziris had said, *is to hide their own vulnerabilities. They like to tickle people because they themselves are horribly ticklish.*

It was a wild idea, but Larkin didn't know what else to do. She loosened her grip on the mangrove root and instead began to tickle it, skimming her fingertips over the reedy roots.

Immediately, the root spasmed and shook, as if with laughter. It released Cordelia, withdrawing back into its island. As soon as Cordelia took in a great gulp of air, Larkin dragged her to her feet and they ran as fast as they could back to the safety of the dock.

CHAPTER NINE

Cordelia and Larkin's mothers, along with a group of other adults who sat on the Glades council, had been sequestered in the living room at Larkin and Zephyr's house, discussing the string of catastrophes that had happened over the last week. The mangrove trying to drown Cordelia had been only the beginning. Dragon-gators had attacked farms, frogres broke into shops, hordes of pix-squitoes descended on people walking outdoors.

The floating market had been closed, school canceled, most houses shuttered, while families hid in darkened rooms, terrified of what waited outside their doors for the first time since they'd followed Oziris into the Glades, believing it to be a peaceful new home.

Everyone was so preoccupied with their own fear that no one noticed Cordelia, Larkin, Dash, and Zephyr hovering outside the living room, listening.

Cordelia had stolen a tall glass from the kitchen and had the mouth of it pressed against the door, her ear to its bottom.

"Do you hear anything?" Dash asked her for the fifteenth time in the last five minutes.

Cordelia scowled at him. "Not with you talking," she snapped, though she knew that wasn't entirely fair. She couldn't hear anything even when he was quiet. Either the door was too thick or no one was saying anything at all. But she'd eavesdropped before and never had trouble hearing, which made her suspect it must be the latter.

"My friend Delvin said that he got *stung* by a pix-squito," Zephyr said. He tried to whisper, but even his whispers were louder than most people's shouts. "He had a mark to show for it, a big bump on the inside of his arm, and he said that for an hour afterward, he was spitting glitter."

"Gross," Larkin said, wrinkling her nose. "I never heard of a pix-squito stinging anyone."

"I never heard of a mangrove trying to drown anyone either," Cordelia said, straightening up and moving away from the wall. She crossed her arms over her chest. "And yet . . ."

She trailed off, but there was nothing more to say, really. The boys already knew about the mangrove attack, even if they didn't quite believe it. Cordelia couldn't blame them—if it hadn't happened to her, if she couldn't still feel the tight grip the mangrove had on her ankle and the water in her lungs, she wouldn't believe it herself.

"Do you think it's because of Dad?" Dash asked. His

voice was barely louder than a whisper. "He died and now everything is bad."

"That's not true," Larkin said, but Cordelia gave a snort.

"That's what everyone's saying," Cordelia said. "And they have a point—the timing can't be a coincidence. My dad was the first human who came to the Glades, he was the one who said it was safe to live here, that we could exist in harmony with all of the creatures here."

Larkin frowned and shook her head. "There must be some other explanation. Our parents will figure it out."

But Cordelia heard only silence from the living room. Their parents didn't have answers either.

Silence stretched over the children as well, no one knowing quite what to say, until Zephyr gave a loud sniffle—a worrisome sound from Zephyr, though not an unusual one.

"Careful," Larkin told him.

"I know," he said peevishly, glowering at his sister. He took a handkerchief from his pocket and blew his nose. Zephyr told them that Minerva had enchanted it for him, a spell meant to trap the magic from his boogers until he got better at controlling it.

Cordelia suddenly remembered an afternoon a few weeks ago when Zephyr had been sniffling beneath a tree while his friends played nearby, his enchanted handkerchief pressed to his nose so hard it was pushed up like a pig's snout. She remembered being a little afraid of him as well, even though she knew she shouldn't have been. Zephyr was her brother in everything but blood, and magical boogers didn't change that.

Her dad hadn't been afraid, though. He'd taken one look at Zephyr from the other side of the clearing and walked straight toward him, his shoulders squared and his head held high. All the other children had watched as the founder of the Glades crouched down in front of Zephyr and spoke to him softly, his expression gentle and kind. And then he drew Zephyr into a hug, wrapping his arms around him and letting him press his face—including that danger-ously snotty nose!—right against his chest.

When her dad drew back and stood up, everyone saw that he was perfectly fine—a fact no one seemed more re-lieved by than Zephyr himself. The other children were a little less afraid of him after that, even though their parents had held on to their own grudges.

Kindness is its own kind of magic. Her father's words from the night he'd died came back to her, making her chest feel tight. But Cordelia knew that no one in the world was as kind as him.

As kind as he was.

Was.

Would she ever get used to saying that?

"Maybe the swamp is sad," Zephyr said after he'd blown his nose. "Maybe that's why."

"It doesn't seem sad, though," Cordelia said, shaking her head. "It seems angry. It seems cursed."

The word hung in the air for a few moments after, echoing in the four children's minds until it became a solid, undeniable thing. A curse. It seemed outlandish and impossible at first, but no more outlandish and impossible than anything else that had happened over the last week. After everything, the idea of a curse made a strange kind of sense, and more than that, it provided a measure of hope in the midst of so much hopelessness. After all, a curse could be broken.

CHAPTER TEN

Cordelia had barely slept since her father died and when she did, she always had the same nightmare—waking up to find out that her mother had died as well. It was a fear that plagued her when she was awake too, though she knew it wasn't a rational one. Her mother was healthy and cautious by nature. The idea of her dying was ridiculous. But then, she'd have said the same thing about her father just last week.

When she'd asked why her father died, her mother had seemed at a loss for words. He'd gone to bed, she told Cordelia, and then he wouldn't wake up. Beyond that, it seemed, there were no answers. And so it stood to reason that the same thing could just as easily happen to her mother, it could just as easily happen to Cordelia herself, or Dash, or anyone.

Cordelia had taken to clinging to her mother whenever she could, accompanying her to the market and on errands—something she hadn't done in years. She even snuck into her bed at night to curl up beside her, counting her heartbeats until she managed to catch a few hours of sleep. Whenever her mother was out of her sight for more than a few minutes, anxious dread began to pool in the pit of her stomach.

So when she woke up in her mother's bed a little after midnight to find her mother gone, cold panic seized her. She threw the quilt off and clambered out of bed, hurrying out the door and down the hall, though still there was no sign of her. Cordelia was just about to run outside when she heard the low murmur of her mother's voice, though it took her a moment to realize where it was coming from. The roof.

Cordelia began to climb the ladder in the hallway, but when she heard her mother say her name, she stopped short, hovering just below the propped-open hatch that led to the roof.

"Cordelia won't let me out of her sight—she hasn't slept in my bed in years, but now she won't sleep anywhere else," her mother was saying, and Cordelia felt a stab of embarrassment.

"It's understandable," another voice said, one Cordelia recognized immediately as Aunt Minerva's. "She's afraid. And she isn't the only one. Larkin and Zephyr have been full of questions, wanting to know what's happening and how we'll fix it."

"What did you tell them?" her mother asked.

"The truth."

Her mother let out a long sigh. "It's a frightening thing, to tell your children you don't know something. It feels like a failure, doesn't it?" She took a shuddering breath. "Oz's death has unleashed havoc. What if we can't stop it without him?"

"We've only just begun to try," Aunt Minerva reminded her, though Cordelia thought she didn't sound like her usual sure self.

"But . . ." Thalia trailed off, gripping the balcony until her knuckles turned white. "He was too young, Minerva, the children are too young, the Glades is as well. If he could be brought back—"

"Don't speak of that," Aunt Minerva interrupted, her voice harsher than she intended it to be, even as Cordelia took another step up the ladder, desperate to hear what her mother had been about to say. "Bringing back the dead is far beyond my magic, Thalia."

"I know that," she said quietly, her voice barely audible even in the still air. "But it isn't beyond Astrid's."

The name hung in the air for a long moment, whispering through Cordelia's mind. It sounded familiar, though she didn't know where she'd heard it before. Whoever Astrid was, it sounded like she had the power to bring her father back to life. The idea of it sparked something in Cordelia's chest. It felt like hope.

For a long moment, Aunt Minerva didn't reply.

"The magic Astrid wields is more trouble than it's worth and it always comes with too high a cost," she said, the words tight. "You know that better than most."

"If there is a cost too high for this, I don't know what it could be," Cordelia's mother said. "If the Glades turns against us—"

"Then we will leave," Minerva said, her voice firm. "We'll go somewhere else, make a new home. We've done it before and we can do it again. As long as we are all together, it doesn't matter where we are."

The words brought Cordelia's fury back to a simmer. They wanted to *run*. To leave behind the Glades—their *home*, the place Cordelia had lived her entire life, the community her father had built from nothing but marsh. They wanted to run away to a place where it was cold for half the year, a place without rivers and marshes, without the Labyrinth Tree and the floating market. Cordelia had only heard stories of the northern lands her parents had lived in before and her father had promised to take her to visit one day, when she was older, but she couldn't *live* there. The thought made her feel sick.

Her father had taught her that running away was never

the right answer. It hadn't been the right answer when one of the older girls in class, Della, called her names and shoved her on the playground last year, and it wasn't the right answer now.

And what was more, there was a way to bring her father back and they wouldn't take it. Who cared what it cost, what the risks were? Cordelia would have found a way to move the earth itself if there was the slightest chance she could see her father again.

Astrid. The name sounded familiar, but only dimly. Larkin would probably know, though. She remembered everything. Somewhere out there was a woman who could bring her father back from the dead. That was all she needed to know to arrive at a decision.

The swamp had taken her father, but it wasn't about to run her out of her home as well.

She straightened up and made her way back downstairs to her bedroom as quietly as she could and began to pack a change of clothes and a second pair of shoes into a cloth bag.

"Whattareyoudoin?" a voice murmured. Cordelia turned to find Dash in her doorway. His eyes were sleep-lined, his dark brown hair mussed and sticking up at all sorts of angles.

"Packing," Cordelia told him. "Go back to sleep."

But Dash didn't listen, instead rubbing the sleep from

his eyes and blinking, as if he thought he might still be sleeping.

"Packing for what?" he asked, watching her stuff a cotton shift dress into a drawstring satchel. "Where are you going?"

For an instant, Cordelia considered lying to him, but what was the point of that? "There's a woman who can bring Dad back from the dead," she told him. "And I intend to find her."

She didn't know what she expected Dash to say to that—to tell her she'd gone mad, maybe, to tell her she was being foolish, to yell for Mom to come and stop her. But he didn't say any of that. Instead, he yawned and stood up a little straighter.

"Then I'm coming too," he said.

CHAPTER ELEVEN

Larkin awoke to someone pinching her arm—Zephyr, more than likely. He'd always been prone to nightmares and would sometimes wake up in the middle of the night, too afraid to be alone.

"You can stay here, Zeph," she said through a yawn, rolling away from the pinching fingers. "Just let me sleep a bit longer."

"Larkin, I need your help," a voice whispered back.

Not Zephyr's voice.

Larkin turned toward it and forced her heavy eyes open to see Cordelia standing beside her bed, silhouetted by the moonlight pouring through the window. She was dressed in her nightgown, a sleeveless cotton shift the color of dead coral, but she was also wearing red rubber boots. There was a satchel slung over her shoulder, stuffed full.

Larkin sat up, blinking. She half expected her friend to

disappear before her eyes, a figment of her imagination, but she stayed put.

"Cor?" she asked, rubbing her eyes. "What time is it?"

"I don't know. Late. Or early, I guess, since it's after midnight," she said. "Who's Astrid?"

Larkin's frown deepened. "Astrid?" she asked, searching her memory.

"She knows our mothers. Some kind of witch, it sounded like?" Cordelia pressed.

"I know I've heard the name, but I can't remember where," she said, shrugging. "Why?"

"Because whoever she is, she has the power to bring back the dead," Cordelia told her. "Your mother said so, but she won't ask her to bring my father back, not even if it saves the Glades."

Larkin straightened, all sleepiness suddenly gone. Just because she couldn't do magic didn't mean she hadn't read every book in her mother's library about it, and she knew exactly what type of magic Cordelia was talking about. "Resurrection magic is dark, Cor," Larkin says carefully. "It's unpredictable and dangerous and it—"

"—always has a cost," Cordelia finished. "That's what your mom said too, but what cost is too high, Lark? To have him back?"

Larkin didn't have an answer for that, but after a moment, she shook her head.

"It doesn't matter," she said. "I don't know who she is."

Cordelia deflated before her eyes, her shoulders slumping forward.

"She's our aunt," a quiet voice said from the doorway. Larkin turned to see Zephyr standing there, in his pajamas, with Dash by his side. "Aunt Astrid. Mama took me to see her last month."

"What are you talking about, Zeph?" Larkin asked. They didn't have another aunt besides Aunt Thalia, and even she wasn't *really* their aunt any more than Oziris had really been their uncle.

Zephyr shrugged. "Mama took me out of school because she said I was sick, but I wasn't. We took a boat across the swamp and then we walked a ways until we came to a little house on the shore. Aunt Astrid was there and she gave me some dust that made me sneeze a lot so she could see what my boogers did. She didn't even seem mad that I melted through her dining table and turned one of her walls purple. Then she gave me lots of chocolate and she and Mama went into the next room to talk for a while. When they were done, Mama took me home."

Larkin and Cordelia exchanged a glance. "I don't know what he's talking about," Larkin said.

"She said not to tell anyone or we would get in trouble," Zephyr said. "She said Aunt Astrid's magic was stronger than hers but dangerous. She said that she might be the only one who could help me control my power—she was the one who made the handkerchief for me and everything. She said that when I got a little older, she would help me control it."

Larkin felt another stab of jealousy at that—her mother had taken her brother to meet their aunt and left her behind because she didn't have magic. It stung. But another thought pierced her: If Aunt Astrid's magic was stronger than even her mother's, could Astrid help Larkin finally reach her own power?

"Do you remember where she was?" Cordelia asked, distracting Larkin from her thoughts.

"No, but it was half a day away and we had to take three different boats," Zephyr said.

Larkin shook her head, hopes deflating. "The boats won't be running their routes, though, not after the marshmaid attacks started," she said. "The entire village is shut down."

"So we'll walk," Cordelia said, as if she were suggesting walking to the floating market rather than across the entirety of the Glades.

"We don't even know *where* we're going," Larkin pointed out.

Zephyr considered this for a moment before furrowing his brow. "Mama had a map. In case we got lost."

"A map," Larkin echoed, feeling a burst of hope. "Do you know where she put it?"

✿

Zephyr found the map to Aunt Astrid's house buried in a drawer beneath a box of tea candles, three pairs of scissors, and too many matchboxes to count.

Cordelia was the one who suggested grabbing some of the other items as well—after all, candles, scissors, and matches were all likely to come in handy on their journey—so she packed them into one of the totes Larkin's mother used for her weekly trip to the market.

Dash had been the one to insist on packing a bag of candy into his own tote, while Zephyr packed a loaf of bread, a few sticks of jerky, and a bottle of water fit with a magical gadget that filtered brackish water to fresh water. The journey had taken Zephyr and his mother only a few hours by boat, but on foot it would take days.

Larkin thought of a few things she might need too, including the dragon-gator scale she and Cordelia had taken what felt like a lifetime ago at the winter solstice party, and a couple of her mother's spellbooks.

In the end, each of them had a tote bag filled with food, clothes, and other necessities to last them the journey. By the time they were finally ready to go, the clock in the kitchen said it was nearly two in the morning.

"That's enough," Cordelia said. "No one will notice we're missing until morning and we'll be too far gone to try and stop."

The four children left the house as the waning moon was high in the sky, each carrying a canvas bag. They made their way through the dark and silent village before setting off into the Glades.

CHAPTER TWELVE

A unt Astrid's house sat on the outskirts of the Glades, across the sprawling Labyrinth Tree, through the winding Wailing Trail, and past Silver Palm Grove. But before Cordelia, Larkin, Dash, and Zephyr could make their way to any of those places, they first had to make it across the Beguilement River.

It was a trip the children had made more times than they could count—for field trips and afternoon picnics and market days and sometimes just for fun—but when they reached the riverbank, they realized that this time would be different.

"Where are all the barges?" Dash asked, looking up and down the river. It was dark as pitch out, but the moon overhead was bright enough that they could see the empty river, running steadily west, and distantly, the opposite riverbank. What they couldn't see were the string of barges tied together that made up the Glades floating market and connected the two banks of the river, forming a makeshift bridge.

Normally, the barges sold everything a person could need: fruit and vegetables, meat, clothing. There was an apothecary barge where people could buy Aunt Minerva's potions, and a fishmonger barge where Larkin and Zephyr's father, Uncle Verne, sold his latest catch when he wasn't at sea. The homewares barge even sold some of Cordelia's mother's pottery, along with things like dishrags, cast iron pans, and scented candles.

Cordelia had spent many weekends walking from barge to barge with her parents and, more recently, alone with Larkin, her allowance tucked away in her pockets, ready to be spent on books or puzzles or sweet treats.

Now all that was gone, leaving Cordelia to realize just how wide the Beguilement River was. She could barely see across it to the other side.

"I heard the market was shut down," Larkin said, squinting into the dark. "But no one said it was *gone*."

Larkin sounded shocked and Cordelia couldn't blame her. The floating market seemed as much a part of the Glades as the mangrove islands or the Labyrinth Tree.

Cordelia led the others along the riverbank before stopping short, her breath hitching in surprise. Larkin bumped into her.

"Oh, bog water," Larkin cursed, her gaze following Cordelia's to what was left of the market barges. They were scattered in pieces—wooden planks tangled in writhing mangrove roots; wet sails blanketed over rocks; tin roofs and support posts barely visible over the surface of the water.

"What happened to all of them?" Zephyr asked, his voice going whisper-quiet.

"Not *all* of them," Cordelia said, shaking her head. "They must have gotten most of the barges out in time. But . . ."

But not these. Cordelia couldn't bring herself to finish the sentence as she looked down at the debris, the sight of it tightening her throat with tears she refused to cry. As they got closer, she could make out more details in the debris— the wooden sign shaped like a pig that had marked the butcher's barge, waterlogged linen shirts from the tailor's barge, and strewn pieces of candy.

No, that wasn't right, Cordelia realized, crouching down to reach into the river and pull out a piece of it. Or, rather, an empty wrapper that had been torn open with something sharp—teeth, maybe, or claws.

Just a few weeks ago, she and her dad had gone to the market together. She remembered him taking her to the candy barge and letting her pick out one of the giant lolli- pops the size of her outstretched hand—a reward for get- ting top marks on a science test. Now it was gone.

"Dragon-gators," Larkin said over her shoulder, and Cordelia felt her stomach plummet, knowing Larkin was right. Dragon-gators had a sweet tooth, but if they came face to face with one now, Cordelia wasn't sure a piece of taffy would be of much help.

Though the thought of dragon-gators worried her, it sparked something else too, something that was becoming a familiar emotion lately. *Fury.* The dragon-gators destroyed this place that held so much of her father, so many of her memories with him. It wasn't fair. The sight of so much destruction hurt her to look at; it made Cordelia want to hurt whatever did it right back.

"We should go home," Dash said, breaking the silence. "Something's wrong."

"That's why we have to keep going," Cordelia replied, crumpling the wrapper in her hand and looking around. "There's got to be another way across."

"We could swim it," Larkin said. "The current isn't strong."

Cordelia shook her head. "Not if we're weighed down with our bags—and even if we did make it, the food and the map would be ruined."

Zephyr scanned the riverbank, watching where the water lapped lazily at the silty earth. It was difficult to see much of anything in the dark, but after a moment, his eyes lit on something. Cordelia followed his gaze.

"Do you see that?" he asked, pointing to the wooden pig sign that had wedged itself onto the bank. "It looks like part of the wreckage, but it might be big enough to hold all of us, like a raft."

"*Might be,*" Cordelia repeated.

"Last I checked, you didn't have a better idea," Larkin pointed out. "And you're the one who said we had to cover as much distance as we could tonight—we're wasting time arguing."

Cordelia pursed her lips and looked at the makeshift raft. "Fine," she said, adjusting her satchel on her shoulder. "But if we sink, I'm going to murder you all."

It was meant as a joke, but the way Larkin, Dash, and Zephyr looked at Cordelia made her realize they thought she just might be serious.

As the four of them made their way down to the raft, Zephyr and Dash paused to break a branch off a nearby cypress tree that looked like it would be long enough to steer the raft with. Because Cordelia and Larkin were the biggest, the boys clambered onto the raft, holding the stick between them, and their sisters pushed them off the shore before jumping on themselves. For a second, everyone held their breath, but the raft sailed out toward the middle of the river and didn't sink.

"Well done, Zeph," Larkin said. "Now, how do we steer this thing?"

Zephyr and Dash managed the steering between the two of them, standing on opposite sides of the raft to keep the weight evenly distributed and passing the stick between them. One would plunge the end of the stick into the water until they hit the river floor, leveraging the raft closer and closer to the distant shore before passing it to the other one to keep them balanced.

While they did that, Larkin and Cordelia sat at the very center of the raft along with the four tote bags they'd brought, trying to keep the weight as centered as possible. The raft felt so flimsy that Cordelia worried that if she were to sneeze, the whole thing might capsize.

They just made it to the center of the river when Dash froze, the stick almost slipping from his hands. "Do you hear that?" he asked, his voice dropping to a whisper.

"No," Cordelia said, frowning, but as soon as the word left her lips, there it was—a voice, singing.

The voice itself was not particularly beautiful—not like Ms. Cavendish, who performed on solstice nights and other events, singing catchy ditties and heartbreaking ballads; not even like Thalia, who would always sing them lullabies when they were younger and could sometimes still be heard singing to herself while she shaped pottery on her wheel. No, this voice was not pretty, but it wedged beneath the children's skin like a splinter all the same. It was the kind of voice that drew blood.

They all went still, the raft also slowing to a near-standstill in the middle of the river. No one dared speak or move or even breathe as the voice came closer. The song it sang had no words, only unintelligible notes that wound their way through the air, inescapable and heady.

The water around the raft rippled and waved and when the singing reached its crescendo, a pair of overlarge eyes appeared beside the raft, set in a face half-submerged in the water, surrounded by tangled waves of seaweed-green hair that glinted in the moonlight.

"A marsh-maid," Larkin said, her voice barely louder than a whisper.

Cordelia didn't correct her, even though the urge to do so rose up in her chest. She had seen marsh-maids before— they all had. Marsh-maids appeared almost human at first glance, but everything about them was too sharp, too delicate, and from the waist down, they were covered in scales of all different colors. But the children had always seen them splashing playfully on the riverbank, singing cheerfully to themselves and waving at anyone who passed by. Marsh-maids were friendly, they were beautiful, they were happy.

The creature slowly rising from the river before them was none of those things, even if she did look physically like a marsh-maid. There was no kindness in her eyes and if she was beautiful, it was in the terrible way that a nightmare might be considered beautiful. The kind of beauty with fangs and claws.

And she wasn't alone. As she rose, her sisters did as well, surrounding the raft on all sides. Cordelia tried to count them, but after twenty, she realized it was a hopeless endeavor and one that didn't matter. They were well and truly outnumbered.

CHAPTER THIRTEEN

Huddled at the center of the raft with Dash, Larkin, and Zephyr, Cordelia watched while the shadowed, over-large eyes of the marsh-maids followed them like they were a chocolate fudge cake. She kept a firm arm around Dash, even when he squirmed to put some distance between them.

"They can't reach us," Larkin said, but despite her words, her voice was sharp and edged with panic, as if she didn't really believe what she said.

She was right, though. Cordelia knew it and Dash and Zephyr surely did as well. The raft was large enough that they were safely out of grabbing distance, and marsh-maids couldn't leave the water. It was something Cordelia thought she'd always known and had only ever questioned once.

She remembered her father, sitting beside her on the riverbank, teaching her to fish, as he shooed away a marsh-maid splashing near them who was in danger of getting tangled in their fishing lines.

"They look like us," Cordelia had remarked. In truth, she thought the marsh-maids were prettier than people ever could be, with their gigantic eyes and high, sharp cheekbones, and long, flowing hair that managed to look perfect even when wet.

Her father had considered the question for a moment. "Marsh-maids are illusions," he said finally. "We see them as human because that is what they want us to see. Watch closely," he said, gesturing to the marsh-maid, who dove beneath the surface of the water. The river was murky and it was difficult to see much of anything, but Cordelia followed her dad's direction. She watched closely.

The marsh-maid swam below their dangling feet, little more than a shadow, but before Cordelia's eyes, the shadow shifted, changed, morphed from something human-shaped to something decidedly not—something squiggly and blobby, without a real shape at all.

"You see?" her father said. "They're as much a part of the river as the water or silt. Just like the river shows our reflection, distorted, so do they. That's why they can't leave the river—it would break the illusion."

Cordelia had taken a moment to absorb this, watching as the marsh-maid's head broke through the surface, with its human eyes and mouth and face. But now that her father had mentioned it, Cordelia could see that those features she thought of as strikingly beautiful looked more like a reflection in a warped mirror.

"Then why do they like to sing so much?" she'd asked.

At that, her father had smiled softly. "They like to sing for the same reasons people do, Cor. Because it allows them to be heard."

But now her father wasn't with her and the song the marsh-maids were singing was unlike anything Cordelia had heard from them before. It was not a song for the sake of simply being heard, it was a song with a purpose—to lure.

Cordelia felt the lure, like a fish who'd caught sight of something shiny, but instead of the promise of food, Cordelia heard a different promise altogether. In the marsh-maids' song, she heard her father's voice, calling out to her.

It was the sound she'd tried so hard to hear at the un-mooring: her father saying her name, over and over again, the way only he did.

Cordelia, Cordelia, Cordelia.

A lump rose in Cordelia's throat and she had to blink away tears. She'd missed that voice so much.

But a voice wasn't enough.

Come find me, Cordelia. I'm waiting for you. I need your help.

A sharp pinch to the soft underside of Cordelia's arm broke through the fog of her mind and she shook her head, trying to clear what was left of it. She looked up at where

Larkin was watching her, gripping her arm like she might pinch it again if necessary, then down at her own feet, horror jarring her fully awake. She'd taken three steps toward the edge of the raft, toward the marsh-maids watching her with hungry eyes. Beneath her feet, the raft tilted, and she scrambled back to the center to keep it from turning over. She knew that if Larkin hadn't pinched her when she had, she wouldn't have hesitated to jump into the water.

Cordelia kept her focus on her friend and not the voices of the marsh-maids who threatened to drown her thoughts once more. *And drown more than my thoughts if I let them,* she thought.

Suddenly, Dash took a step toward the water, causing the raft to lurch perilously again, then another, his face looking like Cordelia imagined her own had looked moments ago— dreamy and heavy-lidded, with a smile stretching across his mouth. Larkin and Zephyr stumbled back to keep the raft afloat while Cordelia lunged toward Dash, but he was one step ahead of her—so close to the water now that if one of the marsh-maids reached for him as the . . . Cordelia didn't let herself finish that thought. If the marsh-maids' singing was loud, then she would have to be louder.

She screamed.

Dash blinked and looked around, as if surprised to find himself where he was. He stumbled back a step, the rocking raft throwing him off-balance, just as a marsh-maid reached out and grabbed at the place where his ankle had been.

The marsh-maids began to sing louder and Dash turned back toward them, his expression already glazing over again, like it did on the rare occasions when he had sleepwalked. Cordelia took a deep breath, preparing to scream again, but before she could, Zephyr launched himself past her and at Dash, tackling him to the raft and pinning him down even as he struggled, putting the raft in danger of capsizing as water splashed around them.

"Cover his ears!" Larkin shouted and Zephyr hurried to obey, but he couldn't manage it. Dash was thrashing so wildly, and every time Zephyr uncovered his own ears, he grew dazed and had to cover them again.

"Dash, it's a trick!" Cordelia yelled. "Cover your ears!"

"No!" Dash said, finally managing to push Zephyr off him, causing the raft to career again, but as soon as he did, Cordelia shoved him back down with her shoulder so that he was sprawled on his stomach at the center of the raft. She kept her hands over her ears and, after a split second of deliberation, sat herself down on his back. Larkin and Zephyr quickly followed suit, piling on top of him so that he had no hope of getting up.

"Let me go!" Dash screamed, kicking his legs and beating his arms to no avail, though the raft continued to rock. "Dad's down there! I have to save him! He needs me!"

"It's a lie, Dash," Cordelia said, but even as she said the words, she could feel her own resolve weakening. What if he *was* down there, waiting for her to help him?

She shook her head, trying to hold on to her sanity. She thought of her real father, his real voice, telling her his last story, about the marsh-maid who couldn't sing.

"Dancing," she murmured, too quiet to be heard over the marsh-maids' singing.

Larkin frowned at her as she struggled to hold Dash down. "What did you say?"

"Dancing," she said, louder. "The marsh-maids love to watch dancing, remember?"

Larkin looked at her like she thought Cordelia had gone crazy. Maybe she *had*, but here they were, stuck in the middle of a river, surrounded by feral marsh-maids. They had to try *something*.

Cordelia gestured for Larkin and Zephyr to get off Dash, but before her brother could scramble to his feet once more and launch himself into the water, Cordelia grabbed him firmly by his hands and began to spin.

It wasn't a graceful dance. While Cordelia was, normally, good at dancing, it was far more difficult to dance on a flimsy raft that wobbled beneath their feet, clinging to a brother who was trying his best to throw himself into the river around them. She had to hold on tight to him and he resisted her at first, his eyes entranced by the marsh-maids watching as they sang.

But something strange began to happen: The marsh-maids stopped their singing. Not all at once, not right away, but one by one their voices faded and suddenly *they* were the ones entranced, watching Cordelia's jerky movements as she twirled her brother around the raft.

When enough of them went quiet, Dash came back to her, and she watched the shock, relief, and fear play over his face as he realized how close he'd come to being at the marsh-maids' mercy.

"Dance," she told him. "As long as you dance, we're safe. Larkin, Zephyr, you too," she added over her shoulder to where they watched, both of them slack-jawed and uncertain.

But they didn't need telling twice. Larkin grabbed her brother's hand and they began to do something that bore a passing resemblance to a waltz, with Larkin having to duck to twirl under Zephyr's arm. It was difficult to dance without tipping the raft over, but with Larkin and Zephyr on one side, and Cordelia and Dash on the other, they managed to keep the raft balanced as they moved very carefully.

"I thought Dad was under the water," Dash said to Cordelia as they danced, his voice a whisper. "I *heard* him."

"I know," she told him, spinning out and then back in the way she'd seen her parents dance at the summer solstice party, both of them laughing and happy. "But they can't have him. He wouldn't let them keep him away from us, you know that. He would fight an army to get back to us—ten armies. A pod of marsh-maids wouldn't stand a chance."

Dash closed his eyes tight, nodding.

"He isn't there, but we're going to bring him back. We can bring him back, but first we have to get through this. Okay?"

For a moment, Dash didn't respond—he couldn't respond, not through the tears coming steadily now—but eventually he managed to nod and began, finally, to dance as well, matching his movements to Cordelia's as best he could.

The marsh-maids' song went altogether silent and Cordelia watched as one by one, they disappeared until none were left and the river was quiet once more. They slowed their dancing and moved back to the center of the raft, watching the river's surface with wary eyes, but the marsh-maids didn't reemerge.

"Where did they go?" Zephyr asked, looking around the dark river.

"I don't know, and I don't want to find out," Cordelia said as she reached for the stick that had rolled to the very edge of the raft. "Let's get across before they come back."

CHAPTER FOURTEEN

The marsh-maids watched the children as they drove their raft onto the riverbank and clambered off, hurrying into the thicket of cypress trees like someone was chasing them.

When they were gone, a deep shudder racked the shoulders of the marsh-maids—if what they had could truly be called shoulders at all. The shudder continued, racing not just through their bodies but through the river itself, and in the pitch-black of the night, the river began to glow a deep, bright gold.

The marsh-maids let out a long, low exhale as one, breaking through the surface of the water and tipping their human-once-more faces up toward the star-cloaked sky.

When they began to sing again, their song was different. No longer haunting or discordant, it was harmonious and hopeful. It was a song of grief and longing, a song that would have brought a person to tears if there had been anyone to hear it, but a song that would have lifted their heart as well. A song that felt like a warm hug and a good healing cry and a sunrise on a new day, all at once.

And as they sang, the Glades around them shivered in a way that was nearly imperceptible, like the hitch in a sleeping kitten's breath the instant before it stretches itself awake.

CHAPTER FIFTEEN

The Labyrinth Tree stretched over an acre of land on the other side of the Beguilement River from the village. In normal times, before Oziris's death, the children visited at least twice a week, either as part of a school trip or for family picnics, or just as a place to play outside after school. With the maze of trunks and the canopy of leaves, it was the perfect place for hide-and-seek.

Now, though, the Labyrinth Tree looked so different from the way it had only a week before, during the solstice party, that it was difficult to believe it was the same tree, the same acre of land that stretched so tall and wide that the night sky above was completely blotted out.

Now, unlike the last time Larkin had been here, there was no music wafting through the air, no thrum of voices murmuring, no people milling around. Now the only sound was the children's footsteps, the only movement the gentle sway of the dangling roots in the breeze.

But it was impossible for Larkin not to see Oziris there, making his way through a thick crowd with a secret smile, shaking hands and making small talk before coming toward them.

I heard there were heathen children causing a ruckus and assumed they must be mine.

Now they were back again, still heathens and causing, quite possibly, even more of a ruckus than before, Larkin thought. The difference this time was that they were no longer his. Oh, she knew they weren't orphaned—they still had three parents between them—but it wasn't the same. There was a part of them now that felt unclaimed. Abandoned.

"I'm tired," Dash said, trailing behind the rest of them, each step dragging as if his feet were made of stone. "Can we stop?"

"No," Cordelia said, not sparing him a backward glance as she plowed ahead. "We're too close to the village—we have to keep going and get as far as we can before anyone realizes we're gone."

"But, Cor, it's so late it's almost early," Dash said, whining like he did only when he was thoroughly exhausted.

"It is late. Early. Both, I guess," Larkin said, her voice coming out tentative. She knew how Cordelia was when she set her mind to something, how impossible it could be to talk sense into her sometimes. But Dash was right, Larkin was tired too; so was Zephyr. She thought Cordelia could do with a few hours' rest herself, though Cordelia would never admit as much. "Maybe a break is a good idea, just long enough for a nap," Larkin continued. "Our moms won't know where we're going for a bit anyways, and then they'll have to cross the river, and we know that's not easy."

Cordelia frowned, but she didn't say no.

"Please please *please*," Zephyr chimed in.

Cordelia rolled her eyes. "Fine. Just for a little bit, until the sun comes up," she said.

They hadn't thought to bring blankets or pillows, but the air was so warm and the ground was so soft that it almost didn't matter. Zephyr and Dash were asleep within moments, their deep, even breathing the only sounds beneath the Labyrinth Tree's canopy.

"Cordelia?" Larkin whispered after a few moments.

"Hmmm?" Cordelia replied, and despite her protests, Larkin could tell she was on the verge of sleep.

"What happens if it doesn't work?" she asked.

Cordelia rolled toward Larkin and leaned on her elbow, propping her head in her palm and opening her eyes to look at her. Her gaze felt like an accusation, and Larkin wished she could take the words back. She didn't know why she'd said them in the first place. *She* wanted Oziris back too, she missed him too—maybe not as much as Cordelia and Dash did, given that he was their dad, but she still felt the loss of him like a gaping hole in her chest. But she'd been disappointed by magic before, most recently here, in the shelter of the Labyrinth Tree, and she *had* to ask.

"It will," Cordelia said, those two words said with enough force to nearly knock Larkin speechless. Almost.

Larkin bit her lip. "Even if we can convince this Astrid woman to help us—and that's a big *if*—that kind of magic is complicated and dangerous and—"

"You don't know anything about magic, Larkin," Cordelia snapped, and that finally silenced Larkin's doubts, or at least drowned them out with different doubts. But no matter how unsure Larkin felt about Astrid or what they would learn when they found her, she couldn't deny that Cordelia was right: Larkin *didn't* know anything about magic, not really.

She knew what she'd read in books, what she'd heard her mother talk about, even what she'd seen her brother do with his, but when it came to magic itself and all its mysteries, what it could and couldn't do, Larkin didn't know anything at all.

Larkin knew this, and had told herself as much, more times than she could count. She was no stranger to her own self-doubt. But hearing it from Cordelia? That hurt worse than Larkin expected. Even after Cordelia's breathing matched their brothers', slow and steady in sleep, Larkin stayed wide awake, staring at the canopy of tree branches, thinking.

CHAPTER SIXTEEN

Just as the sun began to lighten the sky and turn it pink, Larkin had an idea—a wild, wonderful, frightening idea that she couldn't ignore.

Cordelia said Larkin didn't know anything about magic, but that wasn't true. Larkin actually knew quite a lot about magic, even if it was only in theory. Not only did she read every textbook and grimoire in her mother's extensive library, but she'd also listened to everything her mother said about magic, and one thing in particular jumped out: The Labyrinth Tree had magic of its own.

Her mother used its leaves in teas sometimes to cure everything from sleeplessness to anxiousness. She ground up bits of its bark into a powder that cured stinky feet, the flu, and more. She extracted sap to use in any potion that needed a boost in effectiveness.

Larkin had felt the magic herself, even the night of the winter solstice when she'd tried so hard to call on her own power. She felt it now, lying awake beneath its canopy. Larkin looked at the dangling roots, swaying in the faint breeze like tendrils of wavy hair. If she *felt* the magic, then couldn't she use it, like her mother did?

She couldn't brew leaves or grind bark or extract sap, but there was more to the Labyrinth Tree than those things. It wouldn't be pleasant, but it would be worth it.

You don't know anything about magic, Larkin. The echo of Cordelia's words drove her up from where she was lying, careful not to wake up Cordelia or their brothers as she tiptoed toward where their tote bags lay in a pile. She dug through two before she found what she was looking for: the pair of scissors they'd taken from the kitchen.

Larkin made her way through the maze of trunks and dangling roots, looking for just the right one. *Magic is about instincts,* her mother always said, so Larkin trusted hers. She stopped in front of a cluster of roots that ended just about level with her eyes. It would be another decade at least before the roots stretched all the way into the earth and thickened into a new trunk. Another few months or so added to that didn't mean much, in the grand scheme of things, did it?

Larkin told herself it didn't. She reached up and separated one root from its tendril, lifted the scissors to it, placing them about an inch from the bottom, and snipped.

The tree *shuddered*. Larkin felt it, and the echo of it beneath her own skin. But she'd come too far to go back now. She closed her eyes and lifted the root to her mouth, ready to eat it and bracing for what she was sure would be an unpleasant experience.

Before she could get it past her lips, though, the rest of the root cluster dangling in front of her retracted into the canopy above, quick as a snake striking. Larkin's eyes followed it and her body felt cold with shock. She'd never seen the tree *move* like that. Sway in the breeze? Of course. But actually move of its own accord, like a creature rather than a plant? It was impossible.

Only it wasn't; Larkin saw it happen with her own eyes. Which meant that the tree wasn't only alive, it was sentient. Which meant it could feel pain. Which meant ... she couldn't finish that thought. She thought of how she'd cut the root and felt ill.

Her mother had done similar things, though, she told herself. Except that wasn't, technically, true. Her mother had gathered leaves that had fallen, she'd chipped off bark after it was already dead. Even when she'd taken sap from the tree, she'd used special instruments that hadn't left behind a mark when she was done.

Larkin dropped the root, knowing there was no way she could bring herself to eat it now, not if it meant all the magic in the world.

"I'm sorry," she whispered up at the Labyrinth Tree. "I didn't mean . . . I'm sorry. I'm so—"

Larkin never got a chance to finish her sentence. The root tendril darted back down from the canopy, wrapped itself around Larkin's ankle, and dragged her up so fast her head didn't even hit the ground.

She barely had time to scream.

CHAPTER SEVENTEEN

Cordelia awoke to a scream. It took her a moment to remember where she was—the Labyrinth Tree—and why—to bring her father back from the dead. Because he *was* dead, something that still took her a moment to remember each morning.

She blinked the sleep from her eyes and glanced around their makeshift campsite to see Dash and Zephyr sitting up as well, with sleep-mussed hair sticking out in all directions and eyes wide with fear.

The scream pierced the air again. *Larkin's* scream, Cordelia realized, catching sight of the ground beside her where Larkin had been sleeping. She wasn't there. Cordelia got to her feet and followed her friend's footsteps in the dirt to the point where they stopped suddenly. There were other marks there too, lines left behind in the dirt—ten of them. Fingermarks, Cordelia realized with deepening dread. As though Larkin had been dragged away by something or someone against her will.

"Larkin?" Zephyr called, following Cordelia and looking around for his sister with growing desperation. He cupped his hands around his mouth. "Larkin!" he yelled, but no one answered.

There was a rustle in the branches above and Cordelia went still, her eyes darting around for the source of the sound, hoping against hope to see Larkin there, laughing at them for falling for her prank, even though she knew deep down that Larkin had never been the pranking sort.

Instead, she saw one of the root tendrils of the Labyrinth Tree, wriggling like a worm on a hook before shooting toward Zephyr. Without thinking, Cordelia threw herself at him, tackling him to the ground just as the root lashed out, before retreating back into the canopy of branches.

"Run," Cordelia said, jumping up and pulling Zephyr with her. For once, Dash and Zephyr did as she said and they ran, weaving through the countless trunks of the Labyrinth Tree.

"What about Larkin?" Dash asked, looking around.

"We'll get her back," Cordelia assured him. "But we can't help her if it gets us too."

As soon as she said it, another root darted down from the canopy, wrapping around Zephyr's wrist, but Cordelia grabbed his other arm and wrenched Zephyr out of the tree's grasp. When the root surrendered and retreated, Cordelia and Zephyr let out a sigh, but then another root grabbed Dash around the waist and dragged him up.

"Cor!" her brother screamed. Cordelia tried to grab him, but this time, her hands found only air.

"Dash!" Cordelia yelled back, but there was no reply. She took a step toward the direction the tree had taken him, but Zephyr grabbed her hand, pulling her in the other direction.

"Come on," he said. "You were right—we can't get them back if the tree gets us too."

Numb, Cordelia followed Zephyr, her mind spinning. Dash. She'd lost Dash—and Larkin. She'd already lost her father. How could she have been so careless to lose them too?

But she was going to get her father back, she reminded herself, pushing her sadness away before it swallowed her whole. She was going to get her father back and she was going to get Dash and Larkin back too, and no stupid tree was going to stop her.

The Labyrinth Tree is older than anyone in the world, maybe older than anyone in the world has ever been—as old as the world itself, her father had told her once. *It looks like a thousand trees, but it isn't, really. The heart trunk is its true body—the rest are only echoes.*

She remembered how her father had taken her hand and pressed it against the heart trunk, how she could feel the rhythm of a beat deep beneath its rough bark, not unlike the way her own heart beat in her chest.

An idea occurred to Cordelia and she made a sudden right, yanking Zephyr behind one of the Labyrinth Tree's trunks. It looked too thin to be the heart trunk, but she placed her palm on it anyways, to be sure.

She heard a faint thud, dim and distant, but nothing like a heartbeat.

"We have to find the heart," she told Zephyr, who looked at her with utter bewilderment. "That's where it'll take them."

Zephyr nodded slowly, but he still looked confused. "Then what?" he asked her.

Cordelia set her jaw, glancing up at the lush green canopy of the tree—the tree that was as old as the world, according to her father.

"If the tree has a heart, then it can be killed," she said, though the words made her feel sick. The Labyrinth Tree was more than a part of the Glades, it was the very center of it, a place where Cordelia had grown up playing with her friends. She had climbed its branches, hidden behind its trunks, sought shelter beneath its canopy during sun showers. More than that, she knew that medicine taken from its sap and leaves and bark had cured her of countless colds and flus and other bouts of illnesses. The thought of killing it felt like a betrayal, and she wasn't the only one who thought so.

"No!" Zephyr said, eyes widening. "We can't *kill* the Labyrinth Tree!"

"We can if it's the only way to save Larkin and Dash," she told him evenly, because if killing the Labyrinth Tree was a betrayal, it was only because the tree had betrayed them first.

Zephyr frowned, but she could see her words sink in, and after a few seconds, he nodded. "How?" he asked.

Instead of answering, she touched his nose.

"You really are crazy," Zephyr said, taking a step back, but she quickly pulled him back behind the trunk.

"It's the only weapon we have," she told him.

"But I can't control it!" he protested. "And I've never tried to do anything that big before."

"You don't have a choice," she said.

She'd heard everyone coddle Zephyr about his boogers, assuring him that in time, he would be able to control his gift, that he just had to be patient, that he had to practice and learn to trust himself. She felt bad about her bluntness, but there was no more time for patience, and no time for coddling. "You have to try. It's the only way we can save them."

Zephyr looked terrified. "Okay," he said after a second.

"Good," Cordelia said, chancing a glance around the trunk, but there was no sign of wriggling roots.

"It took Dash that way," she said, pointing. "That must be where the heart is. You know how to listen for the beat?"

He nodded and Cordelia wondered if her father had taught him too, the same way he'd taught her.

"Good," she said. "On the count of three, you go that way, I'll go this way. As soon as you find the heart, do whatever you have to do, okay? And if I find it first, I'll shout."

Zephyr nodded again, but he still looked terrified. Cordelia was afraid too, but she was resolved not to show it. Instead, she gave his hand a quick squeeze. "One, two, three."

She and Zephyr ran in opposite directions. Every few trunks, Cordelia paused to lay her hand to them, listening for the heartbeat. The next three she tried were as faint as the first, but the fourth . . . the fourth was louder. Only slightly, but louder all the same. It meant she was getting closer.

Cordelia neatly ducked to avoid one wriggling root sailing toward her and hopped over another that slithered over the ground, checking more trunks as she went, though she realized it wasn't necessary—she could *feel* the heart trunk somewhere deep within her own heart, their rhythms matching.

And then she saw it. There wasn't anything different about it compared to all its shadow trees, nothing that stood out enough to mark it as the heart, but Cordelia knew as soon as she approached, feeling the beat of the tree's heart beneath her own skin like an echo.

"Cor!" a voice called out, and she looked up to see Larkin and Dash hanging high above the heart trunk, tangles of roots around Larkin's ankle and Dash's waist. They were both fine, she saw with relief, though they both looked afraid. There was something else in Larkin's expression that she couldn't place, but there would be time to dwell on that later.

"Hang on," she told them, though she realized how useless the words were as soon as they left her mouth. They had no choice in that—the tree was holding on to them, not the other way around. "Zephyr, over here!" she called out.

She heard Zephyr's footsteps padding toward her from some distance. Looking at the heart's trunk, Cordelia felt a strange pull toward it.

Cautiously, she laid her palm against the rough bark of the tree. The heartbeat grew louder—so loud Cordelia could hear nothing else—but it wasn't only the tree's heartbeat anymore. She closed her eyes, and images darted through her mind: glowing pix-squitoes flittering through the dark, yawning dragon-gators sunbathing, frogres hiding their stolen coins and jewels beneath lily pads, marsh-maids singing far sweeter than Cordelia had heard them before. All their hearts, beating in time with the tree.

But there was something else too, something dark and sticky beneath the surface. *Rot,* she thought.

Cordelia was so lost in listening to the tree that she didn't feel the roots close around her wrist until she was yanked off the ground and into the canopy, between Larkin and Dash. The motion sent a jolt of pain through her arm, like it was about to be yanked out of its socket. A scream escaped her lips before she had even registered what was happening.

"Cordelia!" Larkin said beside her. "Are you all right?"

Cordelia wasn't sure—her arm ached still, but aside from that, she wasn't hurt. Even her wrist, where the Labyrinth Tree's roots wrapped around her, didn't hurt. The tree's hold was firm enough to keep her prisoner, but gentle enough that it didn't bite into her skin.

"I'm fine," she said, which was true enough. She focused on what she'd felt in the heart trunk. "It's sick," she said. "The tree is sick and so is the Glades."

"Cor . . . ," Larkin began, frowning, but Cordelia shook her head.

"I *felt* it. The heartbeats of every creature in the Glades. The tree holds them all."

Which meant that if Zephyr succeeded in killing it . . .

Cordelia watched Zephyr approach the heart trunk, his eyes darting up toward them and widening. Panic coursed through her and she fought against the roots holding her, desperate to throw them off, but they only tightened, digging into her skin.

"Zeph, listen to me," Cordelia shouted down, struggling to keep her voice calm so that she didn't scare him any more than he already was.

"I know," he interrupted, his jaw clenching the way it did whenever he was steeling himself to take a bite of broccoli. "I have to kill it."

Cordelia felt fear flood through her—no, not through her, through the *tree*. She could still feel the tree, deep inside her chest, as if it had dug its roots into her too.

"No," she said quickly, shaking her head. "No, Zeph. The tree is sick, not bad. You need to *heal* it."

That was what Minerva had said, wasn't it? That Zephyr's boogers didn't only have the power to destroy but also to heal?

Zephyr shook his head. "I can't," he said, his voice breaking.

"You can," Larkin said next to her, her voice coming out shaky, but sure. "You have to try, Zephyr. It's what your magic is for—not to hurt but to heal. You just have to believe it yourself."

"But it could hurt you," Zephyr said. "If I try and fail—"

"Better to try," Cordelia said, deciding not to tell him the rest of what she suspected—that if he did kill the tree, he might just kill the rest of the Glades as well. He had enough pressure on him in this moment, and Zephyr had never done well under pressure. Cordelia knew he needed comfort and encouragement, so she put on her best smile and ignored the fear clawing at her as surely as she ignored the grip of the Labyrinth Tree's roots around her wrist. "You can do it, Zeph."

Beside her, Larkin nodded and echoed Cordelia's encouraging tone. "Magic is about intention," she told him. "Mom always says that. You can do it, I know it."

"Let those boogers fly, Zephyr!" Dash added, pumping his fist into the air.

Cordelia wondered if Dash understood how serious the situation was, but perhaps it was better that he was making light of it, especially when Zephyr smiled a little bit in response and the anxiousness in his eyes dimmed, if only slightly.

Zephyr squared his shoulders and turned his gaze to the heart trunk. But he was glaring at it, and Cordelia could feel the hate and anger and fear rolling off him.

Cordelia didn't know much about magic, not like Larkin, but she'd heard Aunt Minerva say that too, that magic was about intention. Right now, Zephyr's intentions were tainted. Just like the Labyrinth Tree was, she realized.

"Wait," she said, and Zephyr's eyes darted up to her again. "Touch it," she said, remembering how it felt to her. If Zephyr could feel what she felt, maybe he would understand. "Put your hand on the trunk."

Zephyr frowned in confusion but did as she said, laying his palm against the bark. Cordelia watched his expression smooth over, his eyes close and his mouth go slack. She felt the tree's heartbeat thunder even louder through her, so loud she was surprised Larkin and Dash couldn't hear it, but all their attention was focused on Zephyr.

When Zephyr's eyes opened again, his expression was clear and his gaze steady. He gave a quick nod that seemed directed mostly at himself. And then he let out a great big sneeze, sending boogers flying all over the heart trunk.

The boogers that had melted Cordelia's birthday cake had been acid green, but these were golden yellow and almost seemed to glow in the faint light of the rising sun. Cordelia found them revolting, but also, in a strange way, inexplicably beautiful.

For a moment, nothing happened. Then a long, deep shudder went through the tree, shaking Cordelia, Larkin, and Dash along with it and making Cordelia feel a little queasy. When the shudder subsided, the roots lowered them very gently to the ground, even taking care to put Larkin right side up.

"You did it!" Dash exclaimed, tackling Zephyr into a hug. Larkin and Cordelia quickly joined in, throwing their arms around their brothers and holding them tight for a moment.

"I did it?" Zephyr asked, sounding a little dazed. "I did! You were right," he added to Cordelia. "When I touched the tree, I felt its rot. So that was what I thought about when I sneezed—how I wanted it to heal. And it did!"

Cordelia grinned at him, though after a second she shoved his shoulder sharply.

"Hey! What was that for?" he asked, rubbing his arm.

"If magic is about intention, then you *wanted* to ruin my birthday cake!" she said.

Zephyr gave her a small, devious grin. "Maybe a little. Dash and I thought it would be funny."

Cordelia opened her mouth to respond, but Larkin interrupted. "Look!" she said, her gaze on the tree.

The Labyrinth Tree's roots had gone mostly still, waving slightly in the breeze, but the heart trunk was glowing, the veins in the bark a pure gold that spread out from the heart trunk, through the branches and into the shadow trunks until the entire tree was aglow, lighting up the darkness all around them.

The four children looked around in wonder, struck still by the beauty of it. Cordelia wished desperately that her father could be here to see it too. The thought jolted her back to her senses. The light was beautiful and bright, yes, but it was bright enough to be seen from the village.

"Hurry, we have to go," she said, starting to walk once more.

"But—" Dash started, frowning.

"The tree just sent up a beacon," Cordelia said. "It's telling our parents where we are. We have to go. *Now.*"

CHAPTER EIGHTEEN

As the children made their way through the Labyrinth Tree, the tree itself listened to them—to the sound of their heartbeats and footsteps and the stories they told one another. The Labyrinth Tree loved stories, after all, and the story the children were playing out now was a good one—if only the tree knew how it ended.

The Labyrinth Tree felt better than it had in days, but it knew it wasn't healed, not completely. Already, it could feel the seed of rot deep within, knew it would fester and grow once more, darker and stickier than it had been before.

A breeze blew through the Labyrinth Tree's branches and the tree gave a great shudder.

CHAPTER NINETEEN

Though the sun was barely in the sky, Larkin followed Cordelia through the now calm Labyrinth Tree, Dash and Zephyr trailing behind and reenacting Zephyr's great sneeze again and again, the excitement driving all the sleep from them.

"What did it feel like?" Larkin asked Cordelia, remembering how her friend's face had gone slack when she touched the heart trunk, like she'd fallen asleep standing up. It was magic, she knew that, and the familiar jealousy nagged at her, but Larkin pushed it away. It wasn't Cordelia's magic, it was the Labyrinth Tree's, and after what Larkin had done, she couldn't blame the Labyrinth Tree for not sharing its magic with her. Besides, if Cordelia hadn't thought so quickly, if Zephyr hadn't managed to control his powers, they all could have been badly hurt or worse. And it would have been Larkin's fault. The knowledge made her feel ill.

Cordelia didn't have to ask what Larkin meant. "It felt weird," she said, shaking her head. For a moment, she didn't elaborate, but finally she sighed. "I felt the Glades—everything from the marsh-malds to the pix-squitoes felt contained in the tree. But . . ." She trailed off.

Larkin didn't press her. A lifetime of friendship with Cordelia had taught her patience.

After a few breaths, Cordelia continued. "I felt my dad too," she said, her voice barely louder than a whisper. "I know it sounds stupid," she added quickly, glancing sideways at Larkin. "I don't know how to explain it. It was like holding his hand again."

"It doesn't sound stupid," Larkin told her before pausing and turning the rest of Cordelia's words over in her mind. "Safe," she said finally. "It sounds like it felt safe."

Magic, Larkin thought again, and she knew she would give almost anything to feel it for herself. *Almost* anything, she reminded herself. She'd realized today what she wouldn't give up—*who* she wouldn't give up.

Cordelia snorted, unaware of the conflict in Larkin's thoughts. "The tree was trying to kill us, but yes, it felt safe too."

Larkin bit her lip, thinking about how the Labyrinth Tree had grabbed her and held her but not hurt her. "I don't think it was," she said. "Trying to kill us, I mean. It didn't hurt me, or you, or Dash. It was just . . . holding on to us."

Cordelia raised her eyebrows. "That's a very generous way of looking at it. If Zephyr hadn't saved us, who knows what it would have done?"

That was just it, though, Larkin realized. They *didn't* know. She wondered if the Labyrinth Tree was aware of what it was doing. She remembered how it set her down, making sure to place her gently on her feet. The gesture hadn't been malicious or even grudging. It had been . . . tender.

"You said it was sick," Larkin said.

Cordelia nodded. "I felt . . . rot in it," she said, frowning. "Zephyr must have healed it."

Larkin thought this over. "I wonder if the rest of the swamp is sick too, not cursed," she said. "You said everything in the Glades was connected to the Labyrinth Tree. If Zephyr healed the tree, do you think he healed the rest of the Glades too?"

Cordelia didn't say anything for a moment. "No," she says finally. "I still felt it, the rot, even after Zephyr sneezed on the tree. It was still there. My dad will know how to get rid of all of it."

Larkin nodded. Of course, Cordelia was right. Oziris would know exactly what to do, he always did, and she knew better than to voice any doubt about the type of magic that would have to be used to get him back again. Like Cordelia said, there was no price too high.

But a few hours ago, Larkin would have said the same thing about getting her magic—that there was no price she wouldn't pay to have power of her own. Now she knew better.

"What were you doing when the Labyrinth Tree got you?" Cordelia asked suddenly.

Alarm shot through Larkin, followed by a flash of shame. Larkin opened her mouth, ready to lie, but she couldn't bring herself to. Not only would Cordelia surely know if she did, but she also just *couldn't*. What she'd done was bad; lying about it would only make it worse. So she told Cordelia everything, about how desperate she'd felt under the Labyrinth Tree, how she'd had a wild idea that seemed good, how guilty she'd felt after cutting one of the tree's roots, and how that had been what awakened the tree.

"You could have hurt yourself," Cordelia told her when she was done, her voice sharp. "You could have hurt *Dash*. Zephyr and me too."

"I know," Larkin said, feeling a quarter of her size. "I *know*. It was a mistake, and the only reason we're all okay is because Zephyr was brave enough to use his magic for good." Once Larkin started talking, she couldn't stop. The next thing she knew, she was voicing something she hadn't even let herself think. "Maybe that's why I don't have magic.

Zephyr's braver than me, and more selfless and just . . . more *good*. He would never have hurt the Labyrinth Tree, no matter what."

Larkin stopped talking when Dash and Zephyr darted past them, running ahead down the path. The last thing she wanted was for Zephyr to hear her talking about that—even Cordelia's hearing it was bad enough.

"Larkin," Cordelia said when the boys were out of earshot once more. "We'll figure out how to get you magic, okay? Once we get my dad back, we'll figure it out. Maybe this Aunt Astrid can help you too."

It was something Larkin had considered too, but now the idea didn't make her happy. It left her feeling hollow and frightened, like when she'd been hanging helplessly in the Labyrinth Tree and watching it take her friends one by one. Because of her.

"No," she said, shaking her head. "I don't want magic." That sounded like the lie it was, so Larkin tried again. "I don't *need* magic."

It was the first time she'd ever spoken those words out loud, and they didn't choke her like she thought they might. She didn't enjoy saying them, but she survived it, and as soon as the words were out, hanging between them, Larkin felt that she could breathe a little easier.

"Remember what your dad said?" she continued. "We all have magic in us—even if it never rises to the surface, it's in everyone, and every*where*. I think . . . I think it's okay if mine stays inside me. I don't want to keep waiting to become someone else, Cor. I want to like who I am."

And the thing was, when Larkin said the words, they felt a little bit true. Maybe that too was its own kind of magic.

CHAPTER TWENTY

Cordelia, Larkin, Dash, and Zephyr walked through the Labyrinth Tree, weaving through its trunks and dangling roots, which had, mercifully, stayed dormant as the children headed west toward Astrid's house. Cordelia felt the Glades waking up as they walked—the sound of the herons and kingfishers in the tree's canopy stirring and taking flight; the ribbits from the frogres with their slimy green bodies and their faces set with overlarge features, sharp teeth, and pointed ears; the buzzing of a swarm of pix-squitoes with their tiny, humanlike bodies fitted with stingers and wings.

The frogres and pix-squitoes didn't attack as Cordelia worried they would, but they didn't wave to the children as they passed either; the frogres didn't try to coax them to join their games, and the pix-squitoes didn't land on their shoulders and whisper jokes in their ears like they used to. Instead, they watched with wary eyes as the children passed.

Whatever Zephyr had done at the Labyrinth Tree had helped, that much was clear, but it hadn't *fixed* everything, and Cordelia couldn't help but feel that whatever improvements they had made weren't going to last. Still, it was nice to feel at peace with her home again, to see the creatures behaving a little more like themselves.

Zephyr and Dash kept running ahead, seemingly full of boundless energy, but they always doubled back a few minutes later.

Every so often, Cordelia took the map from the pocket of her dress, turning it this way and that and nodding as if she understood it, though she wasn't sure she did. The map had made sense when she first looked at it—she recognized certain places, like the Floating Market and the Labyrinth Tree—but beyond that, all the map showed was the Beguilement River, Aunt Astrid's house all the way west, and a path, vaguely called the Wailing Trail, that should have taken them straight to Aunt Astrid's from the Labyrinth Tree. But if a trail ever existed, Cordelia couldn't see it now. All she could see were trees. She wasn't sure the exact moment the shadow trunks of the Labyrinth Tree changed into this forest of cypresses and pines and tupelos, but now she couldn't see any hint of the Labyrinth Tree at all.

One day, the Labyrinth Tree will cover the whole of the Glades, her father had told her. One day, it would come this far and farther. It would always grow, always spread.

At the time, the thought had filled Cordelia with awe. She couldn't have been more than six and had taken the words to have a double meaning—the tree would grow, and so would she. Now, though, the thought was bitter, like a mouthful of tree sap.

It wasn't fair that the Labyrinth Tree still lived and thrived and grew when her father didn't. *She* didn't want to grow without her father.

She pushed the thought aside and focused instead on her next step, and the one after that. Each step brought her closer to bringing her father back.

After endless trees, Cordelia was relieved to see something new flicker to life on the horizon, but when she realized what it was, that relief was replaced by fury.

"The river?" she asked, her voice rising as she fumbled for the map again, unfolding it as if it might have suddenly changed in the last few minutes.

It hadn't. They should have been walking straight toward Astrid's cottage. If they were seeing the river, that meant . . .

"We went too far east," Larkin confirmed, glancing at the map over her shoulder. "But here, if we follow the river, it'll take us to Astrid's as well, and we'll be able to use it as a guide."

"Until the marsh-maids come back, in case you forgot," Cordelia snapped, crumpling the map and shoving it back into her pocket.

Larkin didn't acknowledge her tone, merely turned the words over in her mind. "We can stay far enough from the river to avoid them," she said, and Cordelia hated how reasonable that answer was. "As long as we can see the river, we'll know we're going the right way."

"We've been going the wrong way for *hours*," Cordelia said, unwilling to give up her anger so quickly. "It'll be dark again soon."

Larkin nodded. "Probably," she said. "But we'll only lose more time if we stand here complaining about it."

Again, Cordelia knew Larkin was right, and again that knowledge only made her more angry. She kicked a pebble lying on the ground in front of her, but it was bigger than she'd thought and left her toe aching.

Larkin's gaze followed the pebble before darting back to Cordelia. For a moment, Cordelia expected her to say something snide or stupid—anything to give Cordelia an excuse to let her temper run free—but Larkin only sighed and started walking again, turning slightly north so they were walking parallel to the riverbank, not toward it. She lifted her hands to her mouth.

"Zephyr! Dash!" she called out, but there was no answer. There was no sound at all, even though their brothers had never been quiet in all their lives. Larkin glanced back at Cordelia, a frown tugging at her mouth.

Dread pooled in the pit of Cordelia's stomach. "Dash!" she yelled, even louder than Larkin had. "Zephyr!"

Again, there was no answer. But as they quieted to listen for one, a new sound filled the air, one Cordelia recognized. Her dread turned to ice-cold fear.

It was the sound of a marsh-maid singing.

CHAPTER TWENTY-ONE

Larkin ran toward the bank as fast as her feet would carry her, Cordelia beside her. When Zephyr and Dash came into sight, a scream rose up in her throat—they were crouched beside the water, mere inches from a marsh-maid, whose mouth was open and singing. The boys leaned toward her, and though Larkin couldn't see their faces, she knew they were once more hypnotized by the voice.

She and Cordelia wouldn't reach them in time, not as close as the boys were to the water, so without thinking, Larkin took a great gulp of air and let out a scream that pierced the air and sent a flock of white herons flying from the trees around them. She screamed so loud she hurt her own ears, her throat made raw with the force of it. She screamed, and a half second later, Cordelia screamed as well, their voices loud enough to disrupt the spell the marsh-maid was weaving on their brothers.

Zephyr turned toward them first, his eyes brightening when he saw them.

"Lark—" he began, but before he could finish, Larkin tackled him sideways, shoving his shoulders in the ground to keep him immobile.

"It's not real, Zeph," she told him. "Whatever she's promising you isn't real. Remember?"

"Ow!" she heard Dash cry out behind her as he too was tackled to the ground, by Cordelia.

Zephyr looked up at her, his brow furrowed. But his eyes weren't glazed over, the way Dash's had been when they crossed the river. Instead, he only looked confused.

"Yes," he said slowly. He tried to shove her off him, but Larkin refused to budge. "Larkin, *listen*," he said.

"No," she snapped. "It's all a lie, you know that."

Zephyr shook his head. He reached up and grabbed her face in both of his hands. *"Listen."*

He wasn't entranced, Larkin realized. Not like Dash had been, not like she'd felt herself become, briefly, before she'd gotten hold of herself. He was as lucid as she was.

Larkin relaxed her grip on Zephyr's shoulders, but only slightly, and did as he said. She listened.

The marsh-maid's voice had the same haunting quality it had yesterday at the floating market, that strange note that worked its way beneath her skin, until Larkin could feel the melody in her bones, in her blood. It was just as wordless and enchanting, beautiful and awful and utterly inhuman. But it was different. The song didn't offer her impossible promises, it didn't whisper through her that her magic was there, just beneath the surface of the water, if only she reached for it. It didn't beckon with shimmering fingers ready to grab.

Instead, the song wrapped around her like a pair of arms folding her into a hug. It rubbed soothing circles on her back. It made her eyes sting with tears that fell freely down her cheeks.

Larkin scrambled off her brother, hastily wiping the tears away, but it didn't do any good—her tears kept flowing freely. She'd never cried like this, she thought, not even when her pet cat had died, or when she tried to use magic again and again only to fail and fail and fail. She hadn't even cried like this when Oziris had died.

Larkin cried until her chest and throat ached. She was dimly aware that she had reached out for Zephyr, for Cordelia, for Dash, and she felt their arms around her, their own tears soaking into her skin.

More marsh-maids joined the first, rising in the water around her and singing the same soul-splitting song, their voices harmonized until it was impossible to tell where one voice began and another ended.

It was worse than the last time Larkin had heard them sing. That had been an illusion—a beautiful, frightening illusion, but an illusion all the same. It hadn't been *real*. This was real, and it *hurt*. It hurt so terribly that Larkin wanted to tear her own heart out if it would make it stop. But then the song ended, the marsh-maids falling silent once more, and Larkin felt something unspool deep within her. She took several deep breaths, savoring the looseness in her chest and realizing that the marsh-maids' song hadn't been the thing choking her—that had been there longer, some burden she hadn't even realized had taken up space within her until it was gone.

Something that had been living in her for weeks now.

Ever since Oziris died, a voice whispered in her mind, and she knew it was the truth.

Next to her, Cordelia gave a sniffle. "What *was* that?" she demanded, scrambling back to her feet and turning toward the marsh-maids like she was ready for a fight.

But the marsh-maids weren't giving her one. Instead, they floated in the water, their heads and shoulders bobbing above the surface and their not-quite-human eyes focused on Cordelia, Larkin, Dash, and Zephyr.

These weren't the same marsh-maids they'd seen before, Larkin thought. But they weren't the ones that had populated their childhood either, full of giggles and splashes and lighthearted songs. Larkin didn't know *what* they were, but she knew they didn't mean her or her friends any harm.

Two more marsh-maids emerged from a copse of mangroves, pulling a raft between them, big enough for the four children. Unlike the sign they'd used to cross the river the day before, this was a proper raft constructed of cypress logs bound together with rope.

Larkin exchanged a glance with the others.

"We aren't taking that," Cordelia said, her voice incredulous. "It's a trick."

Larkin looked at their brothers, then at the raft, then back at Cordelia. "I don't think it is," she said, her mind a whirl. She stepped toward the water, toward the marsh-maid lurking closest to them.

"Larkin!" Cordelia exclaimed, trying to pull her back, but Larkin wrenched her arm out of her friend's grip. She knelt down beside the marsh-maid, so that they were nearly eye to eye. Then she held out her hand.

The marsh-maid's strange silver eyes dropped from Larkin's to look at her hand. Tentatively, she reached her own hand, or something that looked like it, out to take Larkin's. As soon as skin touched skin, Larkin's mind was flooded with the sound of a heartbeat, so loud she could hear nothing else. It felt like the thing Cordelia had described when she touched the heart's trunk—the heartbeat of the Glades. Larkin could feel the dragon-gators and the mangroves and the phoenix-flies, all their hearts beating to the same rhythm as her own. And there, under the surface, just like Cordelia had said . . . there was rot.

When she pulled away, she blinked rapidly, trying to understand what she'd seen, and feeling like her body wasn't quite her own. Cordelia, Dash, and Zephyr stared at Larkin as she got to her feet, her legs unsteady beneath her. Cordelia took hold of her arm to steady her.

"It's safe," she told them, nodding toward the raft.

"How do you know?" Cordelia asked, brow furrowed.

Larkin shrugged. "The same way you knew the Labyrinth Tree was sick," she said. "Whatever rot there is, it's below the surface. For now."

Cordelia snorted. "That's not comforting," she said. "It could come back as soon as we're in the lake, and then the marsh-maids will try to drown us all over again."

"Then we'll dance again," Larkin told her. "Wouldn't you rather face a problem you know how to solve than whatever might be lurking if we stay on land?"

Cordelia still looked skeptical, but she didn't argue as Larkin pulled her toward the water, toward where the marsh-maids pushed the raft to meet them. They stepped onto it one by one, first Dash, then Zephyr. It was sturdier than the raft yesterday had been, barely rocking as they moved onto it. When Larkin went to follow, Cordelia held her back.

"Come on," Larkin said, giving her arm a tug. She placed one foot on the raft, then another, but Cordelia's grip kept her anchored to the shore. "Trust me," she said.

Cordelia gritted her teeth and Larkin could see another

protest building in her, but Larkin didn't give her time to voice it. With all her strength, she pulled Cordelia onto the raft, sending them both toppling.

One marsh-maid gave them a shove along the shoreline, and another approached the raft with a stick long enough to reach the bottom of the marsh. Then, as suddenly as they'd arrived, the marsh-maids disappeared once more and the children were alone.

CHAPTER TWENTY-TWO

Cordelia, Larkin, Zephyr, and Dash took turns using the stick to propel the raft down the river toward Astrid's house. Though there hadn't been any further sign of the marsh-maids, Cordelia couldn't stop scanning the water for them. It made her uneasy, this sudden turn in their behavior, and she couldn't let go of the fear that had gripped her when she'd seen Zephyr and Dash at the water's edge, leaning toward the creature.

She couldn't lose them too, she thought, before pushing the thought aside. She wasn't losing anyone. Yes, maybe her father was lost now, but she would find him again. It wasn't a permanent loss.

When the sun set over the mangroves to the west, the children gave up using the stick, laying it down over the raft and settling down to rest in a tight circle, letting the river push them lazily along toward Aunt Astrid's. Cordelia reached into her tote bag to pull out the food they'd brought from Larkin's house—sticks of dried jerky, a few oranges, a bunch of carrots, a loaf of bread, and Dash's bag of candy. They were almost out, she noted, though she didn't say it aloud. She didn't want to worry anyone. And besides, they'd be at Aunt Astrid's soon enough, and surely she would give them food.

As Cordelia took a bite of her jerky, she cast another glance around the marsh, looking for any ripple in the water, any stream of bubbles, any sign of the marsh-maids. Larkin followed her gaze and seemed to know where her mind was.

"I don't think they're going to bother us again," Larkin said.

"But *why*?" Cordelia asked. "It doesn't make sense—they wanted to kill us just a day ago."

Dash shrugged. "You said the Labyrinth Tree was sick," he pointed out. "But it wasn't *just* the tree."

"The tree is the heart of the swamp," Zephyr added.

"I felt it when I touched the marsh-maid too," Larkin said, nodding thoughtfully. "The connection to the rest of the swamp."

"Maybe, when Zephyr healed the Labyrinth Tree, he healed the rest of the swamp too. Maybe everything is fixed now," Dash said.

Maybe we don't need to bring Dad back after all.

He didn't say it out loud, but Cordelia heard it. She clenched her jaw, ready to snap out an answer, but Larkin got there first.

"No, I still felt rot, just under the surface. I think what Zephyr did at the tree was only a temporary fix," she said.

"Well, what if Zephyr sneezed on everything else?" Dash asked before bursting into laughter and nudging Zephyr. "You can just sneeze on everything and everyone!"

Zephyr laughed too and mimed a big sneeze, making both boys laugh even harder. Larkin smiled too, but Cordelia clenched her hands into fists at her sides.

"It isn't a *joke*," she snapped. "None of this is a joke."

"They know that, Cordelia—" Larkin started, but Cordelia didn't want her to keep talking in that calming, reasonable way that made Cordelia feel like a dragon-gator with a thorn in its claw.

"Why am I the only one taking this seriously?" she shouted. Shouting felt good, she realized. It felt like it was releasing something inside her. "It's like none of you even *want* to bring him back!"

"Of course we do," Larkin said, her own voice sharpening. "But Dash is right; it's possible there's another way—"

"Possible," Cordelia said, mocking Larkin's higher-pitched voice in a way she knew somewhere deep down was mean, though at the moment she didn't care. "I'm not about to

risk the Glades for *possible*. You don't know anything, Larkin. None of us knows *anything*. But my dad does, so I'm still going to bring him back. If you don't want to come, you can go back to the village."

"No one said we didn't want to bring Oziris back," Larkin said quickly, her gaze softening, which made Cordelia even angrier. She didn't need pity, not from any of them. "We're in this together."

"We aren't," Cordelia told her, the words rising to her lips before she could think to stop them. "He was *my* dad, mine and Dash's, not yours. Don't act like you understand how I feel because you *don't*. You *can't*."

Larkin opened her mouth to speak but quickly closed it again, looking away, though Cordelia caught the pain in her eyes. She told herself it didn't matter, all she'd said was the truth, but that didn't make the seed of guilt that had taken up residence in her belly go away. The guilt somehow made her even angrier.

"The Glades needs him," Cordelia continued, looking at each of them in turn—Dash, then Zephyr, then Larkin. None of them met her gaze for more than a second, but Cordelia told herself it didn't bother her. *I need him,* she added silently, not trusting herself to say that part out loud. It felt as if saying those words would crack her open.

"Come eat some more, Cor," Larkin said, unable to keep the hurt from her voice, but Cordelia shook her head.

"I'm tired," she said. "I'm going to sleep."

There wasn't much room on the raft, but Cordelia managed to find a place to stretch out, using a folded-up sweater as a pillow. She kept her back to the others, pretending to sleep while they spoke softly. They didn't talk about her father anymore, or the marsh-maids, or even magic, but those were the thoughts that danced through Cordelia's mind, keeping her awake long after the others had joined her, lying down on the raft and settling in to sleep as best they could. Even when the swamp around them had turned as quiet as it could ever be, her mind still shouted.

Cordelia didn't know how long she lay like that, waiting for sleep to claim her. She didn't know when it finally did, or what she dreamed. All she knew was that, when she woke, it was to a bloodcurdling, inhuman screech and the smell of smoke.

CHAPTER TWENTY-THREE

Silver Palm Grove earned its name because of the way the rising sun shone on the small copse of palm trees clustered at the edge of the river, where the water met solid ground again. Larkin remembered her and Cordelia's parents bringing them and their brothers here one morning, just before dawn, to watch as the sun rose over the grove, the palm trees glistening like her mother's jewelry.

She remembered Oziris's low and steady voice weaving a story for all of them, one that had even the other parents hanging on his every word.

Larkin could hear the echo of that story now in her mind, the tale of a dragon-gator who'd placed a bet with a frogre about which of them could jump over the grove's tallest palm tree. The dragon-gator had thought himself clever because he could simply fly over the palm tree, but the frogre insisted that was cheating. After trying for five days, neither of them could manage to jump over the tallest palm tree—the frogre could jump high enough that his toes reached the top of the tree's fronds, but he couldn't propel himself over, while the dragon-gator couldn't get more than a few inches off the ground. Finally, as the sun was setting on that fifth day, the frogre turned to the dragon-gator and said, "If we work together and I jump as high as I can and you use your wings to glide us over, I think we can make it."

And sure enough, the frogre and the dragon-gator worked together, holding on to one another as the frogre jumped and the dragon-gator glided. Together they just managed to sail over the top of the tallest palm tree.

It wasn't a logical story; Larkin had known so even at the age of six. Dragon-gators were much, much bigger than frogres—a frogre couldn't jump so high and manage to lift himself *and* the dragon-gator. But even though she knew the logic was faulty, she still loved the story. Like all of Oziris's stories, she'd been able to see them coming to life around her, in the quiet of the grove, with the sun coming up over the horizon and turning all the palm trees silver.

Now, Silver Palm Grove was not silver, though the sun had barely risen. No, now the palm trees were shades of red and orange and yellow and, in places, burnt black. Now, Silver Palm Grove was on fire.

Larkin watched in stunned horror as a dragon-gator cut

through the sky, its great green wings flapping so hard, Larkin could feel the breeze on her face. That breeze fed the flames, making them jump and grow.

It was a terrible sight to behold, and something deep within her rioted. She had to clench her hands into fists to keep herself on the raft as it floated lazily by. Larkin was vaguely aware of the others stirring around her, but she couldn't tear her eyes away from the blaze.

"So much for it being fixed!" Cordelia shouted, her eyes red, though whether it was from the smoke or tears, Larkin doubted even Cordelia knew.

"It doesn't look fixed," Dash admitted, gaze tracking the dragon-gator across the sky as it swooped down over the palm trees and let loose another gust of flame.

Larkin felt the heat of the fire on her face and wanted to turn away, but she couldn't look away from the flames, the grove where she'd once played now burning to ash.

"The rot's back," Larkin said, her voice small, barely audible over the sound of the fire and the screeching dragon-gator.

"But it won't reach us," Cordelia said, wiping at her tears and straightening her shoulders. "If we stay in the water and sail by—"

"We can't just leave!" Zephyr exclaimed, tearing his gaze away from the raging fire to look at Cordelia, his eyes wide. "We have to help."

"Help?" Cordelia asked, her laugh hard-edged and barely a laugh at all. "What are we supposed to do about it? It's a dragon-gator! Breathing fire! Even if it didn't hurt us, there's no getting close enough without burning ourselves!"

Some part of Larkin knew that Cordelia was right: There was no setting foot in Silver Palm Grove without becoming human barbecue. But it seemed every bit as impossible to stand on a raft and sail by without doing anything to help.

Larkin's eyes found a stretch of sand coming up on their left, far enough from the palms that fire hadn't touched it. *Yet.* If she timed it right, she could jump from the raft and . . .

And what? Even if she did jump from the safety of the raft, even if she did manage to run into the grove without burning herself, even if she did manage to reach the dragon-gator . . . What was she supposed to do then?

Sure, Zephyr had healed the Labyrinth Tree for a time, but Zephyr had magic boogers. Larkin didn't. She didn't have anything at all to help her, just a bone-deep knowledge that she couldn't stand by and do nothing while the dragon-gator raged and the grove burned.

They were approaching the sand bank now, and Larkin didn't have any more time to think.

She jumped.

CHAPTER TWENTY-FOUR

As soon as Larkin stepped into the grove, she felt the heat of the fire on her skin, warm at first, then blazing hot. Her skin felt the way it did after a day outside when the sun had taken its toll, before her mother covered her with aloe gel from head to toe. It didn't quite hurt, not yet, but she knew it was only a matter of time before it did.

Her bare feet sunk into the sand as she ran, looking around for something, though she didn't know what. She felt guided by instinct more than anything now, as if her body were acting on its own and her mind was only along for the ride.

"Larkin!" a voice called behind her. Cordelia's voice, accompanied by the sound of footsteps. "Larkin, come back!"

Larkin's feet didn't listen to Cordelia, though the rest of her was tempted to. A few steps ahead of her, a frond came crashing down from one of the trees, flames swallowing it whole, and when it hit the sand, a sputter of sparks came flying toward her.

Larkin winced, bringing her arm up to her face and bracing for a burn . . . but the burn never came. When the sparks touched her skin, she felt a zap, like when Dash rubbed his hands over a balloon and then poked her—it was a shock, yes, but it didn't hurt. It certainly didn't burn as she expected it to.

"Larkin!" Cordelia's voice came again, more panicked now. "Are you okay?"

"I'm fine," Larkin said, the words awed and more to herself than to Cordelia. She lifted her voice so that her friend could hear her. "I'm fine!" she yelled. "Stay back, Cor, I'm not hurt."

She *wasn't* hurt. Unbelievably, impossibly, *magically* unhurt.

The fire raged on around her. The heat of it still warmed her skin, but it didn't scare her, not anymore. Larkin started walking again and when she reached the fallen palm frond, she couldn't stop herself from reaching out a hand to let her fingertips graze the edge of it, where blue flames licked and spread.

Again, a jolt blossomed beneath her skin, shocking but not painful, and when she pulled her hand back, it looked the same as ever. Not at all like when she was six, when she reached up to touch a pot on the stove when her mother's back was turned. Her skin wasn't red now, it wasn't puckered or scarred. It didn't hurt.

Larkin let out a low exhale, trying to make sense of it, but she couldn't. The fire simply wasn't burning her.

Magic, she thought, the word sending a thrill through her. The magic she'd been waiting so long for, the magic that she'd told Cordelia she didn't even want anymore, though that had, on some level, been a lie. She still wanted it, but she didn't *need* it. She knew she could have been happy without it.

And now it had finally decided to arrive.

A laugh bubbled up in her throat, but it quickly died when a shadow fell over her, casting the space around Larkin in cool darkness. Larkin looked up to see the silhouette of a dragon-gator flying overhead. It let out a shriek that rattled Larkin's bones and released another plume of flame, catching the top of another palm tree.

Larkin took a deep breath and shrieked back, the sound that came from her lips closer to dragon-gator than human. She snapped her mouth shut, eyes going wide. *What was that?*

Stop, she'd meant to say. *Come down here.*

And if that wasn't what she'd said, it seemed to be precisely what the dragon-gator heard. It stared at Larkin with wary eyes as it spiraled down toward the ground and landed a few feet in front of her, its large wings creating enough wind to make Larkin stumble back a step, though she quickly righted herself and met the dragon-gator's gaze.

"Larkin!" Cordelia shouted. Her voice was closer now and though Larkin didn't dare look behind her, she knew that Cordelia had followed her despite her warnings.

"It's okay," Larkin said, keeping her eyes on the dragon-gator and her voice calm. The dragon-gator eyed her mistrustfully, smoke coming from its nostrils as if, at any moment, it might barbecue her. Larkin might not have been burned yet, but she wasn't keen on putting her newly discovered magic to such a deadly test. "I . . . it's listening to me, Cor," she said before hesitating. "*She's* listening to me."

Larkin didn't know how, but she was certain beyond any doubt that the dragon-gator was a girl.

"Larkin, back away slowly," Cordelia said, her voice low.

Irritation prickled at Larkin's skin—Cordelia was so bossy sometimes, but Larkin knew what she was doing. Well, that wasn't technically true. Larkin had no idea what she was doing, but some hidden part of her seemed to know, and she put her faith there. She ignored Cordelia and thought about what she wanted to say to the dragon-gator.

"I'm sorry," Larkin told her, but again the words came out as a dragon-gator shriek. "I'm sorry you're hurt and angry, but you're hurting the trees too. I don't think you want to do that."

The dragon-gator gave a little huff and sparks flew from its snout. Larkin had to force herself not to take a step back. She was aware of Cordelia behind her, but luckily, Cordelia didn't say anything.

"Or maybe you do," Larkin said in her dragon-gator voice, changing tactics, the way she often had to whenever she was navigating one of Cordelia's tempers. "Maybe you're hurting and you want to hurt others. I suppose I understand that. Does burning the grove down make you feel better?"

The dragon opened its mouth and Larkin closed her eyes, bracing to be burned, but instead the creature let out a mournful wail.

Larkin let out a shaky breath. She didn't hear the dragon-gator's wail as words, but she understood the feeling she was conveying, felt the overwhelming grief lurking beneath her anger, the pain she was trying to burn out.

"I know how you feel," she said. "But destroying the grove only makes you feel better for a moment, doesn't it?" she asked. "Then you're sad again. Only now, the grove is sad too, and soon there won't be anything left of it at all. Then how will you feel?"

The dragon-gator let out another keening whine, tossing its head indignantly, and Larkin felt her annoyance and stubbornness, but also a flash of the dragon-gator's shame. Part of her, hidden deep beneath the surface, knew that Larkin was right. Larkin pushed forward.

She set her hands on her hips the way her mother did whenever Larkin or Dash talked back to her. "You'll feel terrible tomorrow when you see what you did," she told the dragon-gator, who ducked her head and didn't reply. "You know I'm right. There's no point in arguing while the grove burns around us, is there?" Larkin asked. "You've made quite a mess, and it's time to clean it up."

The dragon-gator only stared at Larkin, and Larkin was sure that whatever spell had been cast would shatter and the dragon-gator would incinerate her where she stood, any second now. Larkin could see in the depths of her moss-green eyes that the dragon-gator was wavering, that the slightest nudge could tilt her in either direction—toward more destruction, or toward healing.

Larkin remembered the last time she'd seen a dragon-gator, before Oziris had died and the Glades had begun to rot, when dragon-gators wanted nothing more than to sunbathe and . . .

Her hands flew to her tote bag and she opened it quickly, rifling through it while the dragon-gator looked on, equal parts wary and curious. She felt Cordelia watching her too, sure her friend had stayed, even with the danger.

Larkin pulled Dash's bag of candy from her bag, holding it up for the dragon-gator to see. The creature's large tongue darted out to lick at her sharp teeth, her eyes focused on the candy with hunger clear in her gaze.

She took a couple steps toward Larkin, but Larkin stepped back, holding the candy high overhead, even though some part of her knew the dragon-gator had wings and could reach it easily.

"No, not yet," she told the dragon-gator, her voice coming out in a dragon-gator's shriek. "First, you clean up your mess, then you can have candy."

Surely, her mother would have said that bribing the dragon-gator with candy was a morally questionable tactic—not one she'd ever used to get Larkin or Zephyr to clean up their rooms—but it was the only trick Larkin had, so she didn't feel bad about using it.

The dragon-gator hesitated a second longer, her gaze darting from Larkin's face to the bag of candy in her hand and back, before she gave a loud huff strong enough to blow Larkin's hair back and spray her face with dragon spittle. Larkin winced and wiped it off with her sleeve just in time to see the dragon-gator spread her wings and leave the ground, flying over the trees to the water's edge. She crouched on the shore, lowering her head.

"Where's it going?" Cordelia asked, running from her hiding place in the grove to Larkin's side, her shaking hands gripping Larkin's arm.

"I . . . don't know," Larkin admitted, blinking. "Drinking, I think?"

"What did you do? You were making weird noises!"

Cordelia said, looking at Larkin like she'd never seen her before. "That thing could have killed you."

Larkin swallowed, knowing Cordelia was right, but also wrong. "She wouldn't have," Larkin told her. "She never meant me any harm, and the fire . . . the fire didn't burn me. Magic, I think. It must have been magic because I . . . I was speaking dragon-gator." The words sounded every bit as ridiculous when she said them out loud as they did in her head.

Cordelia stared at her, mouth gaping open. "That's not possible," she said after a few seconds of stunned silence.

Logically, Larkin couldn't disagree, but she'd felt the proof of it herself.

"The fire didn't burn me either," she added, holding up her hand to show Cordelia. "I'm not sure why. I don't think being fireproof is linked to speaking with dragon-gators."

Cordelia seemed too stunned to reply, so Larkin nodded toward the sky where the dragon-gator had reappeared. Her eyes found Larkin's again briefly before she turned her attention to one of the palm trees currently ablaze. The dragon-gator opened her mouth again, but instead of fire, a stream of water emerged, dousing the flames.

"Oh my bog," Cordelia said under her breath as her eyes followed Larkin's, tracing the dragon-gator's every move.

"Where are Dash and Zephyr?" Larkin asked as the dragon-gator let another stream of water fly over a second palm, then a third, before returning to the water to refill.

"I told them if they didn't stay on the raft, I would tell all their friends they were so afraid of the dragon-gator they peed their pants," Cordelia said, shrugging her shoulders. "I don't think they believed me, but they didn't really want to risk it."

Larkin laughed, and after a second, Cordelia joined in. They watched as the dragon-gator returned and sprayed a few more trees before repeating the process.

"So," Cordelia said after a minute. "You can speak dragon-gator. I've never heard of a witch doing that, not in any of the stories I've heard, not even your mom. And you're fireproof?"

Larkin couldn't fight a smile as a wave of pride washed over her. "I know I said I was okay without magic—and I'm sure I would have been—but I'm so happy, Cor. Imagine all the good things I can do if I can speak to dragon-gators. And not get burned either!"

Cordelia draped her arm over Larkin's shoulders, pulling her into a side hug as they continued watching the dragon-gator. Half the fire was out now, though many of the trees were scorched black.

"Do you think it's only dragon-gators you can talk to, or other creatures too?" Cordelia asked her.

Larkin considered it for a moment before shaking her head. "I have no idea," she said, unable to resist a grin. "But you'd better believe I'll be finding out."

Cordelia smiled back before surveying the burnt trees.

"I'm glad the fire won't be spreading, but it's too late for most of these trees," she said with a sigh.

Larkin nodded, her eyes following Cordelia's, noting that the trees were now more burnt than not. Her excitement at her newfound magic was drowned out by sadness. This wasn't the place she remembered anymore. She'd been too late—her magic had been too late. At the thought of magic, though, Zephyr came to mind. She turned to Cordelia. "Maybe Zeph can use his boogers to heal the trees, like he did with the Labyrinth Tree!"

Cordelia's eyes sparked. "I'll get him; stay here," she said. "We don't want the dragon-gator to think you ran off with the candy."

CHAPTER TWENTY-FIVE

As the dragon-gator circled in the sky above Silver Palm Grove, putting out the fires it had caused in a fit of a tantrum, its large, glassy eyes kept darting to the girl standing at the center, then at the other three children making their way toward her, through the charred trees and patches of fire still burning.

Seeing the destruction sent a pang of guilt through the dragon-gator—she hadn't meant to do so much damage, but she hadn't been feeling like herself in quite some time and it had felt good in that moment to ruin something beautiful. But then the girl had spoken to her—*spoken to her*! The dragon-gator still couldn't believe it. She took a great gulp of water from the river and put out the last few fires, wondering what it meant.

But the urge to destroy the grove was still there, buried deep within the dragon-gator. She didn't know how long it would stay that way.

CHAPTER TWENTY-SIX

When Cordelia found Larkin again, Zephyr and Dash at her heels, Silver Palm Grove was no longer on fire, though the air still smelled heavily of smoke and scorched coconuts. Larkin was standing right where Cordelia had left her, but now the dragon-gator was perched in front of her, its great wings folded on its back and its snout pressed to Larkin's hand. Even though Cordelia trusted Larkin and her newfound magic, she couldn't help but gasp when the dragon-gator's tongue lashed out to take a piece of taffy from Larkin's fingers.

"Hey!" Dash exclaimed from behind Cordelia. "That's *my* candy!"

"I'll get you some more," Larkin said without looking up as she fed the last piece of taffy to the dragon-gator. Then she reached her hand up toward the dragon-gator's forehead. Bold as she'd seemed earlier when Cordelia had been trying to convince her to run, now she faltered, her hand hovering over the creature's scales. Cordelia thought she saw Larkin's hand tremble as well.

But the dragon-gator closed the distance between them, pressing her forehead against Larkin's palm. At the contact, a shudder ran through Larkin's body and her eyes closed.

"Thank you," Larkin said, her voice whisper-soft, and even though Larkin was no longer speaking in those strange screeching sounds, the dragon-gator seemed to understand her.

Larkin dropped her hand and turned to them, swaying slightly on her feet. In an instant, Cordelia was beside her, reaching out to steady her friend.

"Lark!" she said. "Are you all right?"

"Fine," Larkin said with a smile that morphed into a yawn. "Just exhausted, even though I feel like I didn't do much."

"Magic," Zephyr said solemnly, nodding his head.

"I don't remember you nearly fainting after healing the Labyrinth Tree," Cordelia pointed out.

Zephyr shrugged. "That was only one tree," he said.

"Speaking of, Zeph," Larkin said. "Do you want to try to heal the trees here? It'll be a lot more than one but—"

"It won't bother me as much as the trees are bothered now," Zephyr interrupted. "So long as I can nap after."

As Zephyr and Dash hurried off, stopping at each tree in

their path to blow some of Zephyr's boogers on it, Cordelia led Larkin over to the base of one of the few unburnt trees to sit down. Cordelia had assumed the dragon-gator would take off now, its duty done, but instead, it collapsed onto its belly in the middle of the grove, its eyes on them. Or, more specifically, on Larkin.

Cordelia kept casting Larkin sideways glances, looking for a sign that some vital part of her friend had changed now that her magic had finally come, that something between them had changed. This was it—what Larkin had been waiting for, what Cordelia had been dreading. She was happy for her friend, of course she was, but she couldn't shake the nagging feeling that the wedge in their friendship had just gotten larger, their paths forming a distinct fork.

"You and Zephyr will both need naps, I expect," Cordelia said, pushing the thought aside as she and Larkin watched the first tree Zephyr had blown his nose on began to change, the charred black of its trunk flaking away to reveal a fresh trunk underneath. The damaged fronds fell away as well, and though new ones didn't sprout in their place, not yet, Cordelia knew they would sooner or later. The trees weren't dead, after all. What was broken could mend.

"Better to get a full night's sleep," Larkin said, her voice sleepy though it was just afternoon. "Continue tomorrow."

Cordelia knew that was a smart choice, but still the added delay chafed at her. She wanted to be at Astrid's already—every extra moment they wasted was a moment without her father, and she'd already lived too many of those. It was nearly unbearable.

"We aren't going to lose much more time, really," Larkin said, as if reading Cordelia's thoughts. "The raft would take hours more, but if we leave at dawn, Quince will take us. We'll get to Astrid's a couple hours later than if we'd never stopped."

Cordelia frowned. "Quince? Who's Quince?" she asked.

Larkin nodded toward the dragon-gator. "That's the best I can say her name with a human tongue, at least," she said, shrugging. "It's prettier in dragon-gator."

"Oh," Cordelia said, looking at Quince. The dragon-gator was big enough to carry all four of them, though Cordelia had never heard of anyone riding a dragon-gator before. But if it got them to Astrid quicker, she would try it. "I'm glad you didn't listen to me," she said after a moment. "I would have hated to lose this place too."

"Yeah," Larkin said with a sigh. "I've always loved it here. Your dad did too. Remember when he brought us here to camp after the summer solstice?"

Cordelia smiled. "He strung up hammocks and we fought over who got the purple one," she said.

Larkin laughed. "And your dad settled it by taking the purple one for himself. You were so mad at him."

"I was," Cordelia said before pressing her lips together. It was strange to think about how mad she'd been at him, the things she'd said. She'd told him she hated him, called him a bad father. The thought of it caused shame to burn through her like the dragon-gator's fire. Why had she done that? Had she even apologized? She couldn't remember. "I told him I hated him," she confessed.

"He knew you didn't mean it," Larkin said. "He always called you Hurricane Cordelia."

"Because I left a trail of destruction," Cordelia remembered. "He always said I had to get better at controlling my temper, that one day I'd say something I couldn't take back."

Something twisted in her chest and she felt tears burn at her eyes. There was no point in crying, she told herself. In just one more day, her dad would be back and she could apologize then. And she would never lose her temper again; she swore it silently. Once her dad was back, she would never ever lose her temper again.

Cordelia cleared her throat. "And then Dash dared Zephyr to climb one of the palm trees all the way to the top because he didn't think Zephyr could do it," she said, determined to focus on something else.

"Turns out he could," Larkin said. "But getting down was a bit more complicated."

Cordelia laughed, wiping at her eyes and hoping Larkin wouldn't notice the tears, but of course Larkin did. She put an arm around Cordelia's shoulders. For a long moment, neither of them spoke. And when Cordelia turned her head to look at her friend, Larkin was fast asleep.

CHAPTER TWENTY-SEVEN

When Zephyr finished healing the palm trees, his nose bright red and eyes drooping closed, he collapsed next to his sister where she napped at the base of one of the trees. Even before Cordelia got to her feet, Zephyr was asleep, his head dropping to rest on Larkin's shoulder and letting out a soft snore.

Magic really must take a lot out of you, Cordelia thought, looking around the grove as she began to walk.

The palm trees were still as tall as they had been in her memory, but many of them had lost their fronds in the fire, Zephyr's magic just enough to sprout new baby fronds. They wouldn't be nearly enough to provide any shade for months, maybe years.

Cordelia remembered, suddenly, coming here with her dad a long time ago, when she couldn't have been more than six. She'd been particularly cranky that day, complaining about everything and whining to go home, but he hadn't seemed to care. Instead, he'd sat her down beside him at the base of one of the trees.

She tried to recall the story now—something about a lost pix-squito? Or a talking snake? There was a frightened human man, she thought, though she couldn't remember what had frightened him. The more she tried to recall details, the more they slipped through her mind like fog.

Frustrated tears sprang to her eyes, which only frustrated her more. She kicked a pebble, sending it flying through the grove, ricocheting off one tree's trunk and landing with a thud at Dash's feet.

Dash. Cordelia looked up to meet her brother's gaze.

"Sorry," she said, hastily wiping away the tears that had gathered in her eyes. "Didn't see you."

Dash shrugged and kicked the pebble back toward her. "So. Larkin can talk to dragon-gators?" he said.

Cordelia nodded. "Maybe all creatures, but we don't know yet," she said. "Apparently, magic is exhausting, so she and Zephyr needed a nap. We'll spend the night here in the grove and then Quince—the dragon-gator—is going to fly us to Astrid's house tomorrow."

Normally, the idea of riding on a dragon-gator would have thrilled Dash, but he only nodded. "Okay," he said, before hesitating. "I think a hurricane's coming," he added.

Cordelia frowned. The weather around them seemed fine at the moment. Hurricanes in the Glades were a serious thing. Hurricanes meant school was canceled and windows and doors were boarded up. Hurricanes meant spending days stuck inside while listening to the wind howl. Quite a few times, hurricanes had led to whole houses being knocked down. "How do you know?" Cordelia asked Dash.

"Don't you feel it?" Dash asked, closing the distance between them. "The air smells like it does before a hurricane."

Cordelia took a deep breath in, though she didn't know what, exactly, a hurricane smelled like. Still, she knew what he meant when she focused on the smell of the air itself, underneath the lingering smell of smoke. "Oh," she said. There was something damp about it, something heavy.

"And there's no wind," Dash said. "Which is probably a good thing, because if it was windy, the fire would have spread faster, but . . . Dad always called it the calm before the storm."

Dash was right. Now that he'd pointed it out, Cordelia could feel a storm on the horizon. "We'll be home before it hits," she told Dash, hoping it was true. "Us, Larkin and Zephyr, and Dad too." She shook her head. "If we'd left the grove to burn, we'd be at Astrid's now, probably. Dad might even be back."

Dash considered that for a moment. "Dad loved this place," he told her. "He'd be glad we stopped to save it."

Cordelia knew that made sense, but restlessness and impatience still echoed through her. "I just want this to be over," she told him, biting her lip. "Dad's been dead for a week. A whole week. I don't know how I can survive another day without him." Cordelia closed her eyes, hastily wiping away any tears gathering in the corners of her eyes. She wouldn't cry, not in front of Dash, not in front of anyone—

Arms wrapped around her, jerking her out of her thoughts, and she opened her eyes to find Dash hugging her, his head against her shoulder.

"I know," he said, his own voice quiet and sniffly.

Cordelia froze for a moment, unsure what to do, but eventually she lifted her hand to rub his back. "There's so much I need to ask him," Cordelia said. "So many things he never taught us—remember when he said he'd show us how to drive a fan boat?"

"And cook his secret recipe for redfish," Dash said.

"Shoot a bow and arrow."

"Light a bonfire."

Cordelia blinked. "That one I know," she told him. "He showed me a few months ago, when I turned twelve."

"Really?" Dash asked.

"Yeah, he said he finally trusted I wouldn't burn the village down," she said, laughing. "But clearly, he couldn't say the same for you."

Dash laughed too. "Well, I know how to drive a fan boat," he said. "Dad didn't teach me, but I watched him, and one time Zephyr and I . . ." He trailed off, biting his lip. "Well, we'd get in a lot of trouble if anyone knew, but we managed to drive one without crashing for ten whole minutes."

"That's better than I could manage, probably," Cordelia said, before a thought occurred to her. "Do you remember a story he used to tell, about a talking snake, maybe?"

Dash's eyes lit up. "The talking bogilisk that was far from home," he said.

"Who scared a human by winding its tail around his leg," Cordelia continued, the pieces she'd forgotten coming back slowly.

"And scared him even *more* by opening his mouth and asking him for directions," Dash said.

"The human let the bogilisk sit around his shoulders while he hiked through the uplands and wetlands, following the bogilisk's directions for . . . how long was it?"

"Three days and three nights," Dash said. "And then the snake slithered from the man's shoulders and dove into the sea, but when he emerged again, he'd suddenly grown ten times his size. He turned back to the man and said—"

"We're home now," Cordelia finished, a blanket of warmth settling around her shoulders, the same way it had the first time her father had told it to her. "And that was how the Glades was born."

They stood in silence in the middle of Silver Palm Grove, the distant sound of birdsong the only noise in the still air.

"I always thought the man was Dad," Dash admitted after

a moment. "Every time he told us that story, I always saw his face."

"Me too," Cordelia said, hugging her brother closer. After a moment, Dash wiggled free of her grip and gave a loud huff of a sigh.

"I've never even seen a bogilisk," he grumbled. "Do you think he made them up?"

Cordelia shrugged, though she'd never seen one either, nor had anyone else she knew, apart from her father.

"Tomorrow, you can ask him," she said.

CHAPTER TWENTY-EIGHT

By the time the sun rose over Silver Palm Grove the next morning, the smell of smoke no longer filled the air, though the wind was beginning to kick up, rustling through the new baby palm fronds and causing the thin trunks to bend and sway.

Larkin had slept soundly, despite the hard ground, and it felt like she'd only just closed her eyes when Cordelia was nudging her awake. Dash and Zephyr were already awake and packing up their bags.

Quince was still there, stretched out over the log of a fallen palm tree, her wings fluttering with every deep breath she took.

It hadn't been a dream, Larkin realized when she saw her, her breath catching as the events of the last day came back to her. She tried to feel if there was anything different about her, some nameable thing that had shifted in the last day that marked her as a new person, but she still felt like the same girl she always had been.

Magic is in the air, Oziris had said. *It's in all of us.*

He'd been right—magic had always been inside her, and the fact that it had risen to the surface didn't change who she was. She was still Larkin, and she realized she was happy about that.

She got to her feet, sleep still making her limbs heavy, and made her way toward where Quince rested. She remembered just last week, before the winter solstice, when she'd been terrified of approaching a sleeping dragon-gator. Now she wasn't afraid. She laid her hand on Quince's head and felt the creature stretch awake, her wings unfurling. Her large green eyes opened and met Larkin's and she lifted her head, pushing into Larkin's touch the same way a pet cat might.

"Good morning," Larkin said. Now that she understood how her magic worked, she could feel the words in her throat, how they weren't quite human.

"Are you sure she can take us all?" Cordelia asked from across the clearing. Larkin turned to see her standing with their brothers, all of them eyeing Quince warily. Not that Larkin could blame them—just yesterday, Quince nearly burned down the entire grove. Larkin relayed Cordelia's question to Quince, and the dragon-gator's dark eyes moved from Larkin to her friends and back.

"She says she can," Larkin told them. "As long as we all hold on tight."

The last part didn't reassure anyone, even Larkin, but she knew without asking that Cordelia would be happy to risk plummeting to her death if it meant they got to Astrid's even just five minutes quicker. And for Dash and Zephyr, the risk was a big part of the fun—Larkin was pretty sure they would want to ride the dragon-gator even if they were only going to the market.

"Come on, then," she said, climbing on top of Quince with a little assistance from the Dragon-gator, who offered her wing as a step. "Let's fly."

Larkin was afraid of heights—a fact she realized only when soaring above the tops of the tallest trees, her arms wrapped around Quince's neck so tightly she worried she'd strangle her, and the wind so loud in her ears that her thoughts became a blur.

Zephyr's arms around her waist weren't nearly as tight as they should have been, and her brother let out a whoop of joy when the dragon-gator dropped a few feet, making Larkin's heart stop for a second. The sound she let out was anything but joyful.

She couldn't tell how Dash was doing behind Zephyr, or Cordelia behind Dash, but no one else seemed to be screaming, at least.

After a few moments of climbing into the air, Quince leveled out, her pace slowing to a gentle glide, and Larkin felt herself relax slightly, her grip on the dragon-gator's neck softening.

She took a deep breath to calm herself and noticed the air tasted different this high up.

"Look at that," Cordelia said, her awed voice barely audible. Larkin didn't have to ask what she was talking about.

The Glades spread out beneath them like a painting, all in shades of green—even the lakes and rivers were a dark moss color. There was the Labyrinth Tree, though only the leaves were visible, stretching out more than an acre. There was the floating market, or what was left of it. There were the mangrove islands. Larkin could even see the village from here, so small it reminded her of when she and Cordelia used to play with dolls.

From up there, the Glades was beautiful, but it also looked so fragile, as though she could destroy it all by breathing too hard.

"Larkin," Zephyr said from behind her, his voice full of warning. "Look south."

Larkin frowned, tearing her gaze away from the Glades below to follow his direction. When her eyes met the horizon, she gasped.

Dark gray clouds were rolling in, a near black haze on the otherwise sunny morning. Storms weren't a rarity in the

Glades—hurricanes blew through a few times a year, with nearly twice as many storms that adults deemed *not quite as bad*. Sometimes, after all the wind and rain cleared, the Glades didn't have a mark to show for it, but just as often, the storms knocked over trees, flooded boats, or destroyed houses. Larkin thought of one of the tall palm trees in the center of the village, still alive and growing despite the plank of wood lodged lengthwise in its trunk.

Almost ten years ago, when she was still in diapers and Zephyr was only a few months old, a hurricane had ruined their house, taking the roof off and flooding the living room. They'd moved in with Cordelia's family for a few months while her father rebuilt it.

Storms, she'd learned early, were dangerous things.

She glanced back over her shoulder, her eyes finding Cordelia's. She'd seen the storm too, but her friend didn't look afraid or even wary of the clouds on the horizon. She only looked determined. Cordelia said something to Dash, who passed the words along to Zephyr, who repeated them to Larkin.

"Cordelia says we'll beat the storm."

Larkin nodded, though the lump of worry in her stomach didn't go away. If there was one thing she knew about hurricanes, it was that they didn't fight fair.

CHAPTER TWENTY-NINE

Cordelia wasn't sure how long they were in the air before Zephyr pointed to a small cottage at the edge of the Glades, on a rocky beach where the swamp met the sea.

"That's Aunt Astrid's!" he yelled, his voice mostly lost to the buffeting air around them. Larkin must have heard, though, because she leaned forward and murmured something in Quince's ear. The dragon-gator immediately began to descend and the cottage came into focus.

Half of the small, wood-paneled house was built on a large, flat round of sandstone, while the rest of it jutted over the sea itself, propped up by thick wood stilts at each corner. In the wild winds that were getting stronger with every moment, the house swayed in a way that made Cordelia's stomach churn.

Quince touched down on the beach beside the cottage,

bowing her body down low so the children could climb off her back easily. Larkin gave her head a pat and murmured something Cordelia couldn't decipher. The dragon-gator closed her eyes and curled up her wings, falling asleep immediately.

Cordelia looked toward the cottage, noting the flickering light of a candle in one of the windows, but her feet felt stuck in the sand. Dash came to stand on her right side, Larkin and Zephyr on her left, but none of them went any farther.

"We made it," Larkin said after a few seconds passed. She sounded surprised by that fact, and Cordelia couldn't blame her—there had been times over the last few days when Cordelia had wondered if they would ever make it here.

She forced herself to nod, thinking about the marsh-maids and the Labyrinth Tree and the dragon-gator, how the Glades had seemed to do everything in its power to keep them from getting here. But here they stood all the same. It was like one of her father's stories, where the heroes take on impossible tasks and receive impossible rewards. They'd completed their quest, she thought. Now all they had to do was walk a few steps to Astrid's door to claim the reward they'd earned.

So why did the prospect of closing that distance feel impossible?

"It's dangerous magic, Cor," Larkin said a few heartbeats

later, when none of them moved. "Bringing back the dead, I mean. Every book I've ever read says it's forbidden magic. There's a reason my mother couldn't do it."

"You mean she *wouldn't* do it," Cordelia said, shaking her head and steeling herself. "We've faced marsh-maids and the Labyrinth Tree—you even tamed a feral dragon-gator. Is this more dangerous than that?"

Larkin glanced sideways at her, her brow furrowed. "Yes, I think it is," she said, and soft as her voice was, it grated on Cordelia.

Cordelia whirled to face Larkin, balling her hands into fists at her sides. "We've come this far and you're just going to give up on him, on the Glades?" she demanded.

Larkin didn't flinch from Cordelia's fury. She held her ground. "The Glades is starting to heal," she pointed out. "The marsh-maids and the Labyrinth Tree and Quince— we've seen them heal."

"Temporarily," Cordelia said.

"Maybe," Larkin admitted. "But it's a start, and maybe we don't need . . ." She trailed off, her eyes darting away from Cordelia.

"Maybe we don't need him," Cordelia finished, her voice flat. "That's what you're saying—maybe we don't need him."

Larkin dragged her eyes back to Cordelia's, but she didn't deny it. "It's dangerous magic, Cordelia. That's the reason my mother wouldn't do it."

"You agreed to come!" Cordelia said, unable to stop her voice from rising. Somewhere in the distance, lightning streaked across the sky, chased by a boom of thunder.

"Because I thought it was the only way to save the Glades. But I don't think it is anymore," Larkin said, matching Cordelia's tone.

"I could sneeze on more stuff," Zephyr broke in. "Now that I can control it. That could help!"

Cordelia glared at him, then swung her gaze to Dash, who was unusually quiet. He was staring at his feet, but after a moment, he looked up at her.

"Well?" she snapped at him. "Are you going to let Dad down now too?"

He flinched and some part of Cordelia knew that wasn't fair, but the knowledge was drowned out by the anger vibrating through her.

"I . . . ," Dash started. "I don't know if Dad would have wanted this," he said quietly.

"*Of course* he would have," Cordelia said. Her eyes darted between the three of them and she clenched her jaw, drawing herself up to her full height—the tallest of the group. "If the rest of you want to chicken out, then fine. I'll do it myself."

"Cordelia, wait," Larkin said, but Cordelia didn't listen. She whirled on her heel, away from them, and started stalking toward Astrid's cottage. After a few seconds, the others fell into step behind her, but Cordelia knew they were still hesitant. Well, she'd show them, she thought, squaring her shoulders. When Cordelia convinced Astrid to bring her dad back, they'd be glad she did, and they'd be sorry they ever doubted her.

Before they reached the two steps leading up to the porch, the red door swung open and a woman stepped out, dressed in a plain green linen dress with a gray shawl draped over her shoulders and her golden-blond hair pulled back into a braid so long it reached her hips. She looked like Aunt Minerva and even Larkin a bit, with the same color hair and familiar wide hazel eyes, but she was taller, with long thin limbs that made Cordelia think of a mangrove tree. When she saw the children, she didn't look surprised, merely sighed.

"I was wondering when you four would arrive," she said, placing her hands on her hips and pursing her lips. "Your parents are worried sick—they've sent me five letters in the last two days!"

Cordelia thought of her mother worrying over her and Dash and bit her lip. She hadn't thought about that when she'd left, and felt a stab of guilt at the idea of her mother worrying about them.

"Hi, Aunt Astrid," Zephyr said, dashing up the stairs and throwing his arms around the woman's waist. "You'll never guess what I did—I controlled my magic and healed the

Labyrinth Tree and now Larkin can talk to dragon-gators and—"

"I'm sure it's a fascinating story," Aunt Astrid interrupted, smoothing Zephyr's hair back from his face. She looked away from him and up at the darkening sky, a frown creasing her brow. "You'd best get inside before you tell me, though; the storm is about to break."

She'd no sooner finished speaking than a crack of lightning flashed across the sky and rain began to fall—just a drizzle, but Cordelia knew it would only get worse. Astrid held the door open and the four of them dashed inside. Larkin cast a look over her shoulder to where Quince napped on, seemingly oblivious to the brewing storm.

"Your dragon-gator will be safe," Aunt Astrid told her, laying a hand on Larkin's shoulder. "They're tough creatures, and they've lived through more than their fair share of hurricanes."

Larkin nodded and let Cordelia pull her inside. Astrid closed the door firmly behind them and cast a glance out the window.

"It's going to be a bad storm," she said. "You're lucky you arrived when you did—I wouldn't want to be stuck outside right now. Speaking of, I should let your parents know you're all right."

Cordelia watched as Astrid crossed the room to what looked like the kitchen, her steps calm and measured, the complete opposite of how Cordelia felt. She hadn't come all this way so Astrid could take her time writing a letter.

"We came for a spell," she said, following Astrid toward the kitchen. .

"Yes, yes, we'll discuss that, but first things first," Astrid said, waving a hand. She took a piece of paper from a stack and a pencil from a drawer and began writing out a note.

"The letter can wait," Cordelia snapped.

Astrid set the pencil down and drew her eyes up to Cordelia's. "You must be Cordelia," she said. "And considering the fact that all of your parents are worried you might be dead, I don't think a letter can wait, if it will put them out of their misery one second sooner."

Cordelia didn't reply but gritted her teeth as Astrid picked up the pencil again. She tried to ignore the nagging feeling of guilt—she hadn't wanted to worry her mother, or Aunt Minerva and Uncle Verne, but there hadn't been another option, had there?

As Astrid wrote the letter, Cordelia took the opportunity to look around the place. The house was a single level, and the main room had a kitchen area set up on one side, a plush sofa on the other, and a small dining table and mismatched chairs in between them. Plants covered every available surface, their pots painted with an array of designs in every color of the rainbow. There were more plants than Cordelia could put a name to, some flowering, others green and leafy, and a few with poky needles sticking out.

The unpainted wooden walls were hung with an array of pictures. Glancing at the one closest to her, she gasped, causing Larkin to follow her gaze. Their parents were in the picture, huddled around a woman who must be Astrid, though all of them looked more than a decade younger. She and Larkin exchanged a look, but before they could speak, Astrid cleared her throat.

Cordelia turned back to her just as she folded the letter she'd written into thirds. She went to the kitchen window and opened it. A moment later, a pelican flew in and landed on the windowsill, opening its great beak. Astrid dropped the letter inside, and gave the pelican a few strokes on its head. "You know what to do," she murmured. The pelican closed its mouth and flew off before Astrid closed the window again.

"You speak to animals too?" Larkin asked her, eyes wide.

Aunt Astrid smiled softly and shook her head. "Not really, but they seem to understand me in a very basic way." She paused, eyeing Larkin. "Is that the shape your power took? Your mother and I had a wager going, but it seems we were both wrong."

"I can touch fire and it doesn't burn, either," Larkin added.

"Fascinating," Astrid said, tilting her head to one side. "Tell me, were you with a dragon-gator when that happened?" Larkin began to nod, but Cordelia interrupted.

"Can't we talk about this later? It isn't why we're here," she said, her voice rising.

Astrid's gaze turned to her and she pursed her lips. "You are every bit as impatient as your father was," she said, shaking her head, though a fond smile tugged at her lips.

Cordelia gritted her teeth. "He was not impatient, and neither am I. But we came here for a reason, and you won't even listen!"

Astrid opened her mouth, then seemed to think better of speaking. She looked back to Larkin. "I've heard stories of witches who took on characteristics of creatures they were near—they could speak the language and more. It might be that because the dragon-gator's skin doesn't burn, yours didn't either. It's a rare gift—I don't think there's been a witch in our family who could do it for several centuries. Now," she said, her attention turning back to Cordelia. "For the reason you came." She leaned against the kitchen counter on folded arms, seeming to choose her next words carefully. "I was sorry to hear about Oziris," she said, nodding toward the picture Cordelia and Larkin had been looking at. "We were very good friends, once."

"Once? What happened?" Dash asked. "Did you get into a fight?"

Cordelia wanted to snap at him to be quiet—they'd been here several minutes now and there was still no talk of bringing their dad back! But she found she was curious to hear the answer as well.

Astrid blinked before shaking her head. "No, not really.

We've always had disagreements, but so do all friends. Our lives just went in different directions, I suppose—the same with the rest of your parents. When we came south to the Glades, they wanted to build a community, but I've always preferred my solitude—my magic doesn't make me many friends, I'll admit. We visited each other often, at first, but then you four came along and I became busy with my own things, and visiting became more and more difficult, and those disagreements took up more and more of the limited time we had together. Eventually, it just became easier to stay apart." She paused and Cordelia had to resist the urge to look at Larkin. It was strange to think that people who had been such close friends could simply not see one another for years. She knew that she and Larkin were already starting to grow in different directions, and Cordelia knew that would only get worse now that Larkin's magic had finally come. But Cordelia couldn't imagine how they could grow *that* far apart. The thought of losing Larkin's friendship altogether sent a bolt of fear through her.

"I regret that distance now," Astrid continued, drawing Cordelia back to the present. "I hadn't seen Oziris in eight years—when you four were still so little. There are many things I wish I could say to him now."

"You can," Cordelia blurted out.

Astrid went still, her eyes settling on Cordelia. They were the same color as Aunt Minerva's eyes, the same color as Larkin's—a vivid hazel—and there was something so familiar in that look that Cordelia couldn't place, though it made her uneasy. Astrid took a deep breath and shook her head.

"Your mothers believe you came to me because you overheard a conversation they were having," she said slowly. "They thought you'd be under the impression that I could revive the dead."

Cordelia nodded, not daring to speak.

Bringing back the dead is far beyond my magic, Thalia, Aunt Minerva had said.

I know that. But it isn't beyond Astrid's, Cordelia's mother had replied.

For a moment, Astrid said nothing. She crossed to where a potted plant sat on a small table near the door, a fern with leaves so long they grazed the floor. Astrid reached out and touched one of its leaves with delicate fingers. After a second, the leaf turned brown and wilted, the effect spreading to the rest of the plant in the space of a few breaths.

Beside Cordelia, Larkin gasped, her hand coming to cover her mouth. "You killed it!" she said, sounding as horrified as Cordelia felt.

Astrid nodded, her face impassive as she looked at the plant.

"Watch," she said, reaching out to touch the leaf again. In another moment, the leaf was green and healthy once more, the rest of the fern following soon after. In the space of a few minutes, Aunt Astrid had killed the plant and brought it back to life.

"So you *can* bring back the dead," Dash said, his voice awed. The others looked surprised as well and it occurred to Cordelia that none of them had really believed her when she'd said it was possible, no matter how sure Cordelia had been. But here they were, and it was true, and a jolt of triumph rocketed through her. She grinned.

"See, I told you," she said to the others, but when she looked at Astrid again, the smile slid from her face. Astrid was shaking her head, her expression pained.

"Plants," she said softly. "I can bring back plants. I've even managed a few trees that were rotted to their core, but that is the limit of my magic."

Cordelia's stomach soured and her fists clenched at her sides. Somewhere in the distance, lightning struck. A harsh gust of wind rattled the windows in their frames. Sheets of rain danced against the roof.

"You don't know the limits of your magic if you don't *try*," Cordelia snapped.

"Cor," Larkin said, her hand coming to rest on Cordelia's arm, but Cordelia shook her off.

Astrid's eyes never left Cordelia's face. "Why don't I make us all some cocoa and I'll tell you a story, hmm?" she said, and the tone of her voice only piqued Cordelia's temper.

"I'm not a baby," she said. "You can't bribe me with cocoa and talk to me like I'm one."

A bolt of lightning flashed outside the window, accompanied by the crack of thunder. It was so close the cottage rattled, and Larkin grabbed Dash's and Zephyr's hands in each of hers.

"Cordelia," Larkin said again, but again Cordelia ignored her. She couldn't fight with Larkin anymore, couldn't stand the thought that her friend had been right all along, that there was no hope of bringing her dad back after all. She couldn't accept that, she just couldn't.

"You aren't a baby," Astrid said with another sigh. "But you are acting like one at the moment, on the verge of a temper tantrum."

Cordelia blinked before glowering at Astrid and crossing her arms over her chest. "I am *not*," she said, even though she heard her father's voice in her head.

You've got a temper like a rattlesnake, Cor. It'll get you in trouble one of these days.

But rattlesnakes struck to defend themselves; their tempers had a purpose. Cordelia's anger had a purpose too. She'd come this far to see her father again, and she wasn't going to leave this cottage without him, no matter who she had to sting.

"You could bring him back if you wanted to, but you don't," Cordelia told Astrid. "You must have hated him so much."

The words were meant to wound, and while they didn't hit their mark, Cordelia could tell from the flash of horror in Astrid's face that there was some truth in them.

"I didn't hate Oziris," Astrid said, her voice still annoyingly soft and soothing. Cordelia wanted her to yell, to fight, *something*. "I loved him, just as you do, and that is why I won't attempt to revive him."

"You're a *liar*," Cordelia snapped just as another bolt of lightning struck too close to the house, causing it to shudder once more.

"Cor, Dash is scared," Larkin said, her pleading voice cutting through the fog of Cordelia's fury.

Cordelia glanced toward her brother, who was clutching Larkin's hand tightly in both of his, the knuckles of his fingers bone white and his eyes wide with fear—fear of *her*, Cordelia realized, though she didn't know why.

"She's going to bring Dad back," Cordelia told him. "I promised you that, remember?"

"Cordelia," Astrid said, and now her voice was not calm, not the way a grown-up speaks to soothe a small child. Now, Astrid sounded afraid. Afraid of *her*, for some reason.

Lightning struck nearby again, and this time the window next to Cordelia shattered, glass shards landing at her feet. Larkin and their brothers moved away from her, running behind the couch, where they huddled together.

"You have to bring him back," Cordelia said, not caring

that they were afraid—let them be afraid, let the raging hurricane destroy this cottage, destroy the Glades itself, what did it matter? If her father was well and truly gone, none of it mattered at all.

"I can't," Astrid said, her eyes darting to the window, then back to Cordelia. "Cordelia, you need to calm down—"

"Don't tell me to calm down!" Cordelia yelled. The door they'd walked through mere moments before was suddenly yanked off its hinges as a gust of wind blew into the cottage. The fire in the fireplace sputtered out; the papers on the kitchen counter scattered; one of the potted plants on a shelf fell to the ground, the pot breaking.

"Cordelia, *please*," Larkin said, and Cordelia tore her gaze away from Astrid just long enough to see Larkin holding on to their brothers with all her strength as the wind dragged them all forward toward the open door. "Cordelia, stop it!"

"Stop what?" she shouted, the wind carrying her voice away as soon as the words passed her lips, but Astrid seemed to hear them all the same.

"The hurricane, Cordelia," she said, and though her voice sounded calm once more, Cordelia could hear the fear still lingering beneath the surface. "The hurricane is coming from *you*."

CHAPTER THIRTY

Wind whipped through the air, tangling Larkin's hair and buffeting her skin. As much as she tried to dig her heels into Aunt Astrid's hardwood floors, the wind still pulled her toward the open door. With Dash's arm in one hand and Zephyr's arm in her other, she couldn't hold on to anything, though she wasn't sure what she *would* hold on to. Aunt Astrid's furniture was slowly being pulled toward the open door as well.

The purple paisley printed curtains were horizontal, the curtain rods bowing away from the walls. The clock painted with various birds crashed to the ground, breaking in two. The books that filled Aunt Astrid's bookshelves flew off, one narrowly missing Larkin's face. And in the center of the chaos, Cordelia stood, eyes blazing and fists clenched at her sides.

The wind didn't touch her, Larkin noticed. Not even a single strand of hair was ruffled. Somehow, the air around Cordelia was still.

Magic, Larkin thought, but that wasn't possible. Magic didn't run in Cordelia's family. But as soon as she thought it, she remembered what Oziris had said the night he died: *Everyone has magic in them. Just because it doesn't rise to the surface doesn't mean it isn't there, inside you.* And here it was, rising to the surface in Cordelia.

The hurricane is coming from you, Aunt Astrid had said to Cordelia. It sounded ludicrous, but after everything the last few days had brought, it also didn't. The hurricane was tied to Cordelia's anger, and so there she stood, in the eye of the storm.

Larkin was familiar with Cordelia's little furies, how her temper, once triggered, put her friend in a haze of anger. One time, years ago, Larkin had accidentally broken one of Cordelia's dolls and Cordelia hadn't spoken to her for a week, but a week and a day later, Cordelia couldn't even remember why she was angry in the first place and they'd moved on as if nothing had happened.

It was difficult to speak sense to Cordelia when she was really, truly angry, and Larkin had never seen her as angry as this. But as Larkin felt her own heart thundering in her chest and looked at Dash and Zephyr, both wide-eyed with fear, Larkin knew she had to try.

It took every bit of energy Larkin had to drag herself and the boys through the wind to Aunt Astrid's fireplace, which jutted out half a foot from the wall. It had iron hooks drilled into the brick, meant to hold up a wooden shelf that had already been blown away.

"Hold on," she told them, though she was sure they didn't need telling. She placed both of their hands on the hooks and didn't let go until she was sure their grips were strong. She urged them to the far side of the fireplace, hoping the few inches would shelter them from the worst of the wind. Then she squared her shoulders and faced her friend.

"Be careful," Dash called out, yelling to be heard over the wind even though Larkin was only a step away.

"I will," Larkin assured him. After all, if anyone knew more about Cordelia's temper than Larkin, it would be Dash.

Larkin's muscles ached as she took one step toward her friend. The wind knocked her sideways, and she steadied herself on the back of a sofa. Though the sofa was big enough to seat five comfortably, even it was being slowly dragged toward the open door.

Larkin took another step, then another, feeling like her legs were weighed down by sandbags. The wind dragged at her, pulling at her hair and clothes. Cordelia didn't look at her, all of her focus still on Aunt Astrid, who was caught in the eye with her, standing stock-still, her eyes impassive.

"Cordelia!" Larkin screamed, though the wind carried

away her words as soon as they left her mouth. Cordelia must have heard her, though, because she winced, as if the sound of her name was a physical strike. Still, she didn't turn toward Larkin; all her anger and fury were trained on Aunt Astrid.

"Bring. Him. Back," Cordelia said, her jaw clenched tight around each word.

But if Aunt Astrid felt the force of Cordelia's fury, she didn't show it. She met the hate in Cordelia's eyes with sympathy and, Larkin thought, a touch of guilt.

"I can't," Aunt Astrid said. Not *I won't*. Not *I shouldn't*. *I can't*. It was an important distinction, but Cordelia seemed too wrapped up in her anger to hear it.

"You have to!" Cordelia replied, her voice breaking on the last word, though she still held herself tall and rigid, poised to strike. "The Glades needs him!"

"It doesn't."

It wasn't until Cordelia and Aunt Astrid turned to look at her that Larkin realized she'd spoken the words aloud.

Cordelia shook her head. "The Glades is cursed," she said. "You saw it—"

"The Glades is mourning," Larkin corrected her, taking another step forward until she too was in the eye of the storm, where the air was still. "Just like we've been—they're angry and hurting and sad. But they're starting to get better—with our help."

Cordelia shook her head. "That was *your* magic that

helped Quince," she said. "And . . . and the Labyrinth Tree was Zephyr."

"It was you too," Larkin pointed out, coming to stand at her friend's side. "And the marsh-maids? Your dad's story helped us with them, remember? We didn't fix it overnight, but it is starting to heal."

Just like we are, Larkin thought, but she didn't say that part out loud. Cordelia didn't seem like she was healing— she didn't seem like she *wanted* to heal.

Cordelia's glare sharpened once more, now focused on Larkin. "You don't understand. You *never* understood. He isn't your dad."

Cordelia had said something similar before, wielded those words like a weapon, but they were the truth.

"No, he isn't," Larkin agreed, reaching out to try to take Cordelia's hand, though she jerked away as if Larkin's touch scalded her. Larkin pushed forward. "But I still love him, and I still miss him so much. All the time, Cor."

"No, you don't," Cordelia said, tears leaking from the corners of her eyes. "If you really loved him, you wouldn't give up like a coward. You'd do anything you could to bring him back."

Larkin bit her bottom lip hard enough that she tasted blood. The truth of it rose in her throat, and though she knew Cordelia might hate her for it, she spoke it aloud.

"He wouldn't want this, Cordelia."

Once the words were out, Larkin couldn't take them

back. She didn't know if she would if she could, not even when Cordelia's fury stoked higher, the wind picking up around them. One of the wooden planks that made up the roof of the cottage pried up, then another, then another until Larkin could see the sky above, such a dark gray that it was nearly black.

"You think my dad wants to stay dead?" Cordelia asked, her voice dripping with disdain.

Normally, Larkin might shy away from that voice, especially when Cordelia was in one of her moods. But Oziris never had, she thought. Whenever Cordelia was angry at him, which was often, he met her anger with a smile and a joke and sometimes with consequences—sending her to her room or taking away her dessert. But he'd never backed down.

Cordelia is like a rattlesnake when she's angry. It's how she defends herself, Oziris had told Larkin once, when Cordelia had been so angry at Larkin that she'd cut their sleepover short, throwing Larkin's pillow and blanket out of her room just after dinner. Oziris had sat with her for an hour until she and Cordelia made up again. *Sometimes you have to show the rattlesnake you mean no harm. And sometimes, you have to rattle back.*

Larkin hadn't understood at the time—after all, Oziris had always been there to smooth things over, so Larkin hadn't *needed* to understand. But now he wasn't. Aunt Astrid couldn't bring him back. And that meant Larkin needed to learn how to rattle on her own. So she held her ground and met Cordelia's glare.

"I think he lived a good life," Larkin told her, surprised at how level her voice came out. "I think he loved you, and Dash, and Zephyr and me as well. I think he would have loved to see us grow up and It isn't fair that he won't. It isn't *fair*, Cordelia, but it's life. And Oziris understood that. Even though he isn't here, he shaped you—shaped *us*—and we'll always be his heathen children, causing a ruckus," she said, smiling at those last words as she remembered Oziris at the winter solstice party, when he'd meant to scold them for misbehaving but instead had been proud of them for protecting Zephyr.

Cordelia smiled a little too, her eyes still shiny with tears. Larkin could see the anger in her, simmering close to the surface, but it was fading, and the winds around them were quieting too.

"I don't know who I am without him," Cordelia admitted, her voice a whisper.

Larkin took the final step toward Cordelia, folding her into a hug and letting her friend bury her face in Larkin's shoulder.

"You're Cordelia," Larkin told her, hugging her tight. "And you get to choose who that is."

When the hurricane's winds quieted enough, Dash and

Zephyr rushed toward them, throwing their arms around Larkin and Cordelia, and the four of them held one another close. Larkin looked up at the broken roof, at the gray sky above, and watched as the golden sun broke through the clouds and began to shine once more.

CHAPTER THIRTY-ONE

A unt Astrid's cottage was well and truly ruined. Half of the roof had been torn off, her furniture was overturned, her collection of potted plants was mostly shattered, and the sheets of rain that had poured in left everything drenched.

"I'm sorry," Cordelia told her as all of them did their best to tidy up, though it seemed to Cordelia that cleaning up the cottage was like sweeping a dirt road—it didn't do much good. She was in the kitchen with a broom and dustpan while Larkin reshelved the fallen books and Dash and Zephyr righted the furniture. Aunt Astrid saw to her plants.

"It's all right," Aunt Astrid told her with a smile so kind it made Cordelia's heart hurt. She still couldn't believe that *she* had caused so much damage. And they'd only seen the house! Who knew how much harm Hurricane Cordelia had caused the rest of the Glades? It seemed impossible, but Cordelia had felt it within herself, felt her anger growing and how it had fed the storm, how the storm in turn had fed her anger. She didn't understand it, but she couldn't deny it either.

Cordelia watched as Aunt Astrid picked up one of her plants from its shattered pot, setting it on the counter and then gathering up the broken ceramic shards. As she held the broken pieces of the pot in her hands, they began to come together, fitting like puzzle pieces until the pot was whole once more.

"You fixed it," Cordelia said, awed.

Aunt Astrid smiled, but it was a sad smile. "Come closer," she said and Cordelia obeyed, leaving aside her broom and dustpan for a moment. The woman placed the pot into Cordelia's hands, and when Cordelia took a closer look, her eyes widened.

The pot wasn't fixed, not entirely. The places where it had broken were still visible, emphasized by thick black lines that wiggled like worms.

"My gift," Aunt Astrid explained, taking the pot from Cordelia and leading her toward the fern she'd demonstrated her powers on earlier. When Cordelia looked closer at the leaves, she saw those same wriggling black lines. "I can destroy things, and yes, I can fix them, but they are never the same. With objects or even plants, those changes are superficial, but when a heartbeat is involved, it changes so much more."

"You said you never tried it on a person," Cordelia said, frowning.

Aunt Astrid bit her lip. "Not a person, no," she said with a sigh. "A cat I had as a girl. Meadow. She died not long after I came into my power. She was old and it was her time, but still I was heartbroken. I thought I could bring her back, and I did. In a sense. She woke up, she walked around, she ate her food and slept and lived, but not really. She wasn't her. She had no interest in the toys and treats she'd once loved, no interest in me even. She was a shell of herself, breathing and alive, but not truly living. Bringing her back wasn't fair to her."

Cordelia didn't say anything, though she understood what Aunt Astrid was telling her. She tried to imagine her father coming back like that—the same face without his smile, the same arms without their warmth. She tried to imagine what it would do to her if her father didn't know her, if his eyes met hers and were empty. She couldn't hold back a shudder.

"I'm sorry for your loss, Cordelia," Aunt Astrid said, putting a hand on her shoulder.

Cordelia had heard those words countless times since her father's death, so many times she'd begun to hate them. They were hollow words, said out of duty, repeated so often they lost any meaning they might have once held. But after the events of the day—of the past few days—and coming from someone Cordelia knew to truly be sorry, those words wedged beneath her skin.

"I'm sorry for your loss too," Cordelia said, because Aunt Astrid had loved her father as well, and no one had been able to acknowledge that loss or comfort her. "I'm sorry I said that you hated him," she added, remembering how that barb in particular had hurt Aunt Astrid.

For a moment, the woman didn't say anything, instead busying herself with picking up another fallen pot and mending it.

"I didn't hate your father," she said after a moment, choosing her words carefully. "But we often disagreed."

"About what?" Cordelia asked.

"Everything—books, food, music. Sometimes I felt like if I said the sky was blue, he would say it was green. He couldn't help it and I suppose I couldn't either. The last fight we had, the biggest fight, was about the Glades. We were new here then, and the peace between the people and the creatures felt tentative. I wanted it to just be the five of us—your parents, Larkin and Zephyr's parents, and me—but Oziris disagreed. He thought we should welcome anyone who sought a new home, that we should create a community."

Cordelia thought of her father, how he presided over council meetings and settled disputes between neighbors, how every weekend when they went to the market, he made conversation with every person who crossed his path, listening to their troubles and triumphs. It seemed exhausting to Larkin, but he had always smiled and said it was part of his duty as the founder of the Glades.

"I was right to leave," Aunt Astrid continued. "I don't think I could have been happy surrounded by so many people, and I know that my magic tends to make people uncomfortable and, like you, angry when it isn't enough." Cordelia felt a stab of shame at that, but Aunt Astrid pressed on. "But your father was right too. Right to build a community that welcomed everyone. At the time, it seemed like only one of us could be right, and we let that drive a wedge between us that never healed. That's what I regret."

Cordelia thought about Larkin, how often the two of them argued over things small and big. She tried to imagine a fight big enough that they would never move past it. Maybe two weeks ago, Cordelia would have thought it was impossible, but now? Now she understood how that could happen, how things could be said that couldn't be taken back. She wondered if it was already happening between them, if it would get worse now that Larkin had magic. If their lives were destined to go in different directions and, one day, they might not intersect at all. The thought made Cordelia want to cry.

Aunt Astrid smiled softly and squeezed Cordelia's shoulder, drawing her out of her thoughts. "You remind me of him, you know," she said. "I think he would be very proud of you—though likely a little angry too, since you did run off into the Glades without telling your mother."

Cordelia winced. Her mother must have been worried sick. Suddenly, she wanted nothing more than to throw herself into her mother's arms and stay there for hours.

As if Aunt Astrid could read her mind, she laughed. "I'm sure your mother is on her way," she said. "Not even a fearsome hurricane could keep her away from you and your brother."

Cordelia nodded, but something was still troubling her.

"What about the Glades?" she asked. "Larkin said she thought it was healing from the curse, or whatever it is, but I can't shake the feeling that it isn't. Not fully."

Aunt Astrid bit her bottom lip, but didn't immediately reassure her, which was all the proof Cordelia needed that she was right. With one last look around the cottage, Aunt Astrid sighed. "Come on, children," she said, clapping her hands to get their attention. "I appreciate the effort, but there's little help tidying can do given the state of this place. And I want to show you something."

❦

Aunt Astrid led the four children out of her house and down the porch steps, past where Quince still dozed, seemingly unbothered by the storm, and walking them around to the rocky shoreline where a rickety wooden deck extended into the sea. Cordelia was surprised to see that it still stood, especially since it looked frail enough to break if she breathed too hard in its direction.

As they walked, Aunt Astrid spoke. "Your mothers told me about the curse, as you called it, but they didn't need to—I'd been seeing its effects for myself, even out here. A swarm of pix-squitoes tried to attack me, and a frogre broke into the cottage and stole all my silverware." Aunt Astrid stepped onto the dock and gestured for them to follow.

Cordelia exchanged a look with Larkin, who seemed to have the same reservations about the dock's strength that Cordelia had, but Dash and Zephyr ran ahead without fear, leaving Larkin and Cordelia no choice but to follow.

"I tried to use my own gifts to fix whatever was broken in them, but it didn't do any good," Aunt Astrid continued as they walked. When they reached the end, where the dock met black water, Aunt Astrid turned back to them. "And then there was Aziel, of course," she added.

All four children exchanged a glance.

"Aziel?" Dash asked. "Who's Aziel?"

At that, Aunt Astrid looked surprised, her dark brows arching up and her mouth forming a small o. "Did Oziris never mention him?" she asked. "Aziel is the bogilisk, of course."

CHAPTER THIRTY-TWO

"The . . . the bogilisk?" Larkin asked, though she'd heard Aunt Astrid perfectly well. Bogilisks weren't real; everyone over the age of five knew that. They appeared in the same kind of made-up stories as lost princesses and castles made of ice and talking animals—though that last one, at least, Larkin had to reevaluate now.

"There's no such thing as bogilisks," Zephyr said matter-of-factly, though Larkin noted that Cordelia and Dash exchanged a look she couldn't decipher.

"I think Aziel would beg to differ," Aunt Astrid said. "As far as I know, there is *a* bogilisk, singular, though I've hardly seen every creature in the Glades, let alone the world. There could be millions of bogilisks out there for all I know."

"Next you'll be telling us unicorns are real too?" Cordelia asked, and though she tried to sound sarcastic, Larkin heard a real question in her friend's voice.

Aunt Astrid smiled. "If they are, I've yet to see one, but wouldn't that be something?" she asked before turning to Larkin. "Normally, Aziel comes and goes as he pleases, but if my instincts are right, you can call for him."

"Me?" Larkin asked, taken aback. "I've only talked to Quince. I don't know how to speak . . . bogilisk," she added, feeling ridiculous even saying the words.

"I'd imagine it's much the same," Aunt Astrid said. "You don't actually speak dragon-gator, do you? You simply speak, and the words come out as they need to in order to be understood."

Larkin hesitated, but Cordelia gave her a little push forward. She swallowed and stepped up to stand beside Aunt Astrid near the water. She took a deep breath and closed her eyes, as if she was steadying herself, but really she was terrified. Every time she'd *tried* to use magic, she'd failed. The only time she'd managed to do it was entirely an accident. What if she failed again now? What if her one burst of magic was little more than a fluke?

She swallowed, feeling the expectations of her friends weighing heavy on her shoulders. When she forced her mouth open and said Aziel's name, it left her lips as little more than a whisper. Nothing happened.

"He's likely quite far away," Aunt Astrid said, undaunted. "You'll have to yell."

Larkin bit her lip before doing as her aunt suggested, yelling Aziel's name as loud as she could. So loud it made her throat hurt. So loud the herons nesting in the mangroves dispersed in a flutter of white wings and disgruntled cries.

The sea stayed relatively calm and Larkin's heart sank. Unlike the solstice, though, or the many, many attempts that had come before, Larkin didn't feel like crying or running away. She didn't feel that same shame wrap around her or embarrassment color her cheeks.

She had tried and she had failed, but she had *tried*.

"I don't want to see a stupid bogilisk anyways," Larkin said, turning around to face her friends again, but they didn't look disappointed. Instead, they stared at her, slack-jawed and wide-eyed. "What?" she asked.

"Larkin, you . . . *hissed*," Cordelia said.

"More of a screech, really," Dash added.

"It was *very* loud," Zephyr assured her. "I don't know how he didn't hear it."

Larkin blinked. It had worked? She felt that she'd spoken normally, but she'd thought she'd spoken to Quince normally too. She turned to Aunt Astrid, frowning, and her aunt laid a hand on her shoulder.

"As I said, Aziel comes and goes as he pleases. Maybe he didn't feel like being summoned."

"Maybe he's like Cordelia," Dash said with a grin. "And he's grumpy about being woken up."

Cordelia glared at her brother and gave his shoulder a

shove, but there was no real anger in it. She turned to Larkin and opened her mouth to speak, but before she could, her gaze shifted to something over Larkin's shoulder and her eyes widened.

"Lark . . . ," she said, and Larkin spun to see what had captured her attention.

The calm waters had begun to churn, waves frothing and crashing against the shore and the dock, splashing them. A sliver of gold slithered over the waves in the distance before disappearing. A moment later it reappeared a little closer and Larkin could just make out a shimmer of scales.

"Ah, there he is," Aunt Astrid said. "I'd hoped his curiosity would win out."

The bogilisk came closer and closer before his golden head finally breached the water's surface just in front of the dock, splashing Larkin as it did.

When Larkin had heard stories of the bogilisk before, she'd always imagined a great big snake, but that wasn't quite right. The creature was shaped like a snake, with a long body that was only just visible beneath the water's surface and tapered into a thin forked tail that jutted up above the waves, but it had a head that more closely resembled one of the dinosaur illustrations in her schoolbooks, complete with bared, sharp teeth, large black eyes, and a row of pointed fins that ran from his forehead down along his back. From far away, his scales had appeared gold, but now that he was closer, Larkin could see that they were myriad colors, flashing and reflecting like rainbows.

It eyed her with those dark eyes and Larkin had the feeling he was measuring her up. She drew herself up to her full height even though, beside him, she felt like a pix-squito.

"Hello," she said, trying to sound less frightened than she felt. It would have been all too easy, she knew, for the bogilisk to open his mouth and swallow her whole. Instead, he tilted his head to one side and continued to survey her.

"What do I say?" she whispered to Aunt Astrid, who glanced back at the others.

"Cordelia had a question. You might want to start there," Aunt Astrid said.

"I did?" Cordelia asked, frowning. "Oh! About the curse? I wanted to know if it's really truly broken now."

Even though Larkin had told Cordelia the Glades was healing, the truth was she didn't know for certain. She asked Aziel anyways.

For a moment, the bogilisk blinked, his dark gaze darting from Larkin to the others. He spoke without a sound, without even opening his mouth, but Larkin felt the words in her mind, clear as anything, and she relayed them to the others.

"More than a decade ago, a man came here from the frigid north, seeking a new home for himself and his friends," she translated before pausing. "I think he's talking about Oziris."

The bogilisk inclined his head in what Larkin thought was a nod before his words filled her head once more.

"He braved the wilds of this land, surviving tricky mangrove roots and marsh-maid songs and wild dragon-gators and more." Larkin paused again. "Aziel is saying he guided Oziris."

"Like Dad's story!" Dash exclaimed. Cordelia shushed him, but her eyes were bright too. Larkin wasn't sure what story they were talking about, but the bogilisk began to speak again before she could ask.

"While others had come before the man, they had sought to destroy these things, seeing only the danger in them. Every strike they made against the land and its inhabitants was repaid tenfold and those intruders were always sent running. Oziris was different—he didn't fear the land, not even when it tried its best to frighten him. Oziris learned to love the land, which he called the Glades, and the land began to love him back, slowly but surely."

The others had gone silent now and Larkin's own heart was hammering away as the bogilisk's story continued.

"Eventually, he brought his friends, who brought their friends, who brought their friends, and the humans settled in the Glades. Children were born, elders died, and there was peace between them and the creatures who had called the Glades home before it had ever been called by that or any name."

Larkin knew what was coming next, could feel the *but* coming. Her throat tightened. She forced herself to keep translating.

"But one day, many years later, Oziris breathed his last breath, suddenly and unexpectedly. The humans mourned, but so too did the creatures, who had loved Oziris in their own way and grieved him in their own way, with fury and ferociousness. The wildlife of the Glades raged and wailed, keen on wrecking the land and themselves in the process, until four children came along."

"That's us!" Zephyr exclaimed. Cordelia clamped a hand over his mouth, but her eyes were round as lily pads, fixed on Larkin with her mouth agape.

"The children were grieving too," Larkin continued as Aziel kept telling his story. "They couldn't believe Oziris was dead. They were angry about it, they were sad, and like the creatures of the Glades, they were, at times, destructive themselves. But as they made their way across the home that had become a dangerous world, the creatures of the Glades recognized them.

"Oziris might not have had enough time to teach the children everything he wanted to, but he taught them to be clever, he taught them to be brave, and he taught them to be kind. It was these things that the creatures recognized, for it was these things the creatures had loved so much in Oziris."

Larkin felt her throat tighten as she relayed the words, but the bogilisk wasn't done speaking. His next words dripped down her spine like ice.

"Still, it wasn't enough."

"What does that mean?" Cordelia asked, her gaze darting from Larkin, to Aunt Astrid, to the bogilisk and back

Aunt Astrid frowned, but she gave no answer.

"If the Glades is mourning, like we are, then it'll heal," Larkin said to the bogilisk. "It's already healing—like the Labyrinth Tree and the marsh-maids and Quince."

The bogilisk blinked those enormous dark eyes at her and, without warning, lunged forward, his tongue darting between his teeth. Out of instinct, Larkin raised her hands, but the bogilisk's tongue licked her palm.

Color exploded behind Larkin's eyes, and images flashed through her mind. She saw the marsh-maids in the Beguilement River, clustered together and singing their terrible song once more, their eyes nearly black despite the bright afternoon light. She saw Quince waking from her nap with a furious roar that shook the earth, smoke curling from her nostrils as she took to the sky. She saw the Labyrinth Tree's branches writhing, wrapping around someone's arm, someone's leg, just as it had done to her, Cordelia, and Dash, only this time it was their parents who were caught by the tree—Larkin's mother and father and Aunt Thalia fighting the roots' hold to no avail. She *felt* the rot that Cordelia had mentioned before, lurking beneath the surface of everything in the Glades.

"We have to help them," Larkin said, her voice shrill as she reeled away from the bogilisk.

"Help who?" Cordelia asked, her own voice rising.

"Our parents—the Labyrinth Tree has them. They must have gotten caught on their way here."

"That's not . . . that can't be true," Cordelia said, looking to Aunt Astrid, whose brow was creased in a frown as she looked at the bogilisk.

"Aziel sees many things," she said. "The past, present, and future all at once."

A dragon-gator's cry—Quince's cry—broke the air, just as it had in the vision Aziel had shown her.

"Quince is feral again too," Larkin said. "So are the marsh-maids—so is everything, I think."

"So the curse isn't broken," Cordelia said, glaring at Aziel.

Larkin began to translate, but it seemed Aziel understood Cordelia perfectly and began to speak once more in Larkin's mind.

"Grief has broken the heart," Larkin translated, frowning as she spoke the words. She opened her mouth to ask what that meant, but before she could, Aziel ducked below the surface again and the only sign of him was the flick of his golden tail above the water's surface as he swam away.

"*Grief has broken the heart,*" Cordelia echoed, watching him go, with her mouth hanging open. "That's all you can give us?" she yelled.

"We have to get to our parents," Zephyr said to Aunt Astrid. "I healed the tree once, I can heal it again."

"Maybe Larkin can communicate with the tree too!" Dash put in. "It's a living thing, after all."

"Grief has broken the heart," Larkin said again, looking to Aunt Astrid. "Oziris called the Labyrinth Tree the heart of the Glades. If it's a tree, you can heal it, can't you? Our magic wasn't enough before . . . but maybe yours is."

"I'm not sure," Aunt Astrid said tentatively. "But I'll do my best."

"We all will," Cordelia said, turning back to face them, her eyes fierce and blazing.

"But how do we get there?" Larkin asked. "Quince is . . . well, she's not herself right now," she said.

"I have a fan boat," Aunt Astrid said. "Come, there's no time to waste."

CHAPTER THIRTY-THREE

A unt Astrid's fan boat was just big enough, barely, for the four children to huddle together on the bow while Aunt Astrid drove it along the coast, weaving between mangrove islands and sandbars that had popped up when the tide went out. The large fan behind Aunt Astrid whirled, too loud to talk over and propelling them forward fast, though Cordelia felt that it wasn't fast *enough*. She wished she could snap her fingers and they would be at the Labyrinth Tree, but that wasn't possible, and logically, she knew the fan boat was getting them there quicker than any other possible option.

Hang on, Mom, she thought, staring ahead as Aunt Astrid turned the boat left into the estuary that led to the Beguilement River. A moment later, Cordelia saw the remains of Silver Palm Grove on her left, blackened tops of the palm trees stretching toward a sky still clouded with smoke.

"Quince!" Larkin exclaimed, barely audible over the sound of the boat's fan, but Cordelia saw her point at the sky above the grove, where she could make out the shadow of the dragon-gator circling. Cordelia held her breath, waiting for the dragon-gator to let loose a stream of fire, now that she'd gone feral again, but she didn't. She merely circled the grove.

"What's she doing?" Cordelia asked Larkin, who looked at Quince with a deep frown furrowing her forehead.

"Waiting," Larkin said after a moment, shouting to be heard. "She wants to finish what she started yesterday, but she also doesn't. She's confused."

Confused was better than angry, Cordelia thought. She only hoped the confusion held until they could heal the Labyrinth Tree once and for all.

How? A voice in her head asked, but Cordelia shoved it aside. Aunt Astrid said she didn't know if her healing power would work on such a large tree, but Cordelia had to believe that it would. The alternative was impossible to imagine.

CHAPTER THIRTY-FOUR

It was surprising how fast the trip to the Labyrinth Tree seemed in the fan boat. The journey that had taken them two days on foot sped by, and Larkin watched as the cypress trees that lined the Beguilement River blurred past. She tried to focus on what lay ahead, but some small part of her was back in Silver Palm Grove, watching Quince circle overhead, confused, angry, and afraid. Still, Larkin knew the best thing she could do for Quince—for all the creatures of the Glades—was to heal the Labyrinth Tree.

As soon as Larkin spotted the first branches of the Labyrinth Tree ahead, with their roots dangling down from their mossy branches, her breath caught and she reached for Cordelia's hand, squeezing it. They were almost there now.

After a second, Cordelia squeezed her hand back. They hadn't really talked about Cordelia manifesting a hurricane, or the cruel things she'd said to her friend. Larkin knew Cordelia might still be mad at her too, somewhere deep down. She couldn't shake the feeling that there was a river running between them, one that was getting wider with each passing day. Maybe that was how Aunt Astrid had felt, when her friends' lives started going in a different direction from hers.

It was a scary thought—nearly as scary as the Labyrinth Tree looming ahead. Its dangling roots were twisting like they were blowing in the wind, but the leaves were still— there wasn't even a breeze.

Larkin swallowed and steeled herself.

"We have to find the heart," Cordelia said, and despite the loudness of the fan propelling them beneath the canopy of the Labyrinth Tree, Cordelia's voice sounded strong and sure.

"It was on the right bank!" Dash shouted.

Aunt Astrid heard him and gave a nod, steering the fan boat to the right and getting as close to the shore as she could.

Larkin, who had helped her dad dock his fishing boat more times than she could count, jumped onto the shore and motioned for Aunt Astrid to throw her a rope, which she secured to the closest cypress trunk. That done, the other four piled out of the boat.

"We should split up," Cordelia said, her wary eyes on

the dangling roots overhead. They weren't trying to grab for them—not yet—but Larkin could still feel the place on her left ankle where they'd grabbed her before. "Do you all know how to listen for the heart?"

Everyone nodded—even Aunt Astrid, which shouldn't have surprised Larkin, though it did. She wondered if Oziris had taught her to do it too. Or maybe, she thought, Aunt Astrid had been the one to show Oziris how to do it. She was the one with plant magic, after all.

"What then?" Dash asked, unsure.

Cordelia opened her mouth to answer, then closed it again before forcing herself to speak. "Then we save our parents," she said, as if it were that easy.

Dash seemed to know better than to press for details.

"Be careful of the roots," Larkin told Aunt Astrid, who frowned, her eyes darting up tracking their movement in the still air. "They'll grab you if you let them."

"They're calm now," Zephyr pointed out. "Not like before."

Well, this time no one cut them with scissors, Larkin thought, though she was too embarrassed to say that out loud. Cordelia looked at her, though, and Larkin flushed red, knowing her thoughts were running along a similar path.

"That won't happen again," Cordelia said, giving Larkin a reassuring smile. After a second, Larkin smiled back. "Stay quiet as you can, and don't touch the roots—only the trunk, when you're listening for the heartbeat," Cordelia added.

Everyone nodded.

"Shout when you find it," Cordelia added and then they were off.

CHAPTER THIRTY-FIVE

Cordelia thought it would be easier to find the heart trunk of the Labyrinth Tree the second time around, but she was wrong. There was nothing familiar in the webbing trunks and dangling roots. It was, as its name implied, a labyrinth, and Cordelia was hopelessly lost. She couldn't trust her memory, and she was too afraid of waking the roots to risk laying her hand on any trunks to feel for a heartbeat—she had to trust her instincts.

She stopped running and stood in the middle of the grove, closed her eyes, and listened. There was the rustle of the branches above her head, the sound of the others' footsteps on the dirt, the caw of a heron somewhere in the distance. And there, coursing underneath it all, was the faint thud of a heartbeat. Cordelia didn't hear it so much as she felt it beneath her skin, matching her own.

She opened her eyes, turned right, and picked up her pace. Now that she'd heard the heartbeat, she could focus on it even as she ran, listening to it growing steadily louder as she wove her way between the Labyrinth Tree's many trunks, ducking to avoid hitting any of the longer clumps of dangling roots.

She caught sight of a trunk ahead of her, one that looked at first like any other trunk, but once she saw it, she couldn't look away. It drew her attention so surely it might as well have been screaming. That was it, she knew—the heart trunk.

She was about to call out when a root snaked down from above and grabbed at her arm. Cordelia managed to duck and roll just in time to avoid it, her shoulder crashing into the dirt, sending a dull ache through her body.

Oh no, she thought, looking around at the tree's roots stirring to life. She'd gotten too close, she realized. The tree didn't want her to get to its heart.

Well, that was too bad. She pushed herself to her feet once more.

"I found it!" she called out as loud as she could, just as another root came darting toward her. This time, though, she was ready and dodged to the side to avoid it before running toward the heart trunk as fast as she could.

"Cordelia?" a voice called out, and Cordelia's heart leapt in her chest. Even though it had been only three days, she realized how much she'd missed the sound of her mother's voice. She squinted up into the tree's branches but couldn't see anything more than shadows.

"I'm here!" she called out. "We're all here! Hang on!"

"Cordelia, it isn't safe!" Aunt Thalia's voice joined in. "Get out of here before it gets you too."

"Been there, done that," Cordelia muttered under her breath as another root grabbed at her arm. She swatted it away. When she reached the heart trunk, she wrapped her arms around it, holding it tight while she waited for the others. Her arms didn't come close to reaching around the whole thing, but she had enough of a grip on it that when the roots darted down, they couldn't grab any part of her.

"Cor!" Larkin called from behind her and Cordelia managed to turn her head just enough to see Larkin sprinting toward her, darting away from roots that tried to grab her too. When she was close enough, Cordelia reached out to grab her, pulling her the last few inches to the tree's trunk.

"Can you talk to it?" Cordelia asked her. It was a wild idea, but they didn't know the extent of Larkin's powers.

Larkin frowned and Cordelia could tell the idea hadn't occurred to her. "Try," Cordelia urged her. "If the others can't get close enough . . ."

Larkin nodded, turning her face to the tree and closing her eyes, pressing her forehead against the tree's bark.

"We're trying to help you, please," Larkin said. Unlike

when she'd spoken to the dragon-gator and the bogilisk, her words came out perfectly understandable to Cordelia. But beneath Larkin's words, Cordelia heard the rhythm of the heart trunk, how it slowed down ever so slightly at the sound of Larkin's voice before picking up again.

"I don't think it worked," Larkin said, frowning.

Cordelia shook her head, understanding dawning on her. "I don't think it needs to—I think it hears us already, without your magic."

Larkin's eyes widened.

Cordelia could hear other sets of footsteps approaching, but the roots were getting more desperate. Cordelia *felt* the desperation in them. She turned back to the tree and pressed her cheek to the rough bark.

"Please calm down," she said. "We're trying to help you, if you could let us."

Again, the tree's heartbeat reacted to her words, slowing slightly but not enough. It still felt erratic and upset and . . . and afraid, she realized. The tree was afraid.

What would her dad do, if he were here, she wondered. But as soon as the thought came, she knew the answer. She knew what her dad always did when *she* was afraid or upset. He would tell her a story.

Cordelia searched her mind for a story—any story— but none of the ones her father had told her felt quite right. A thought occurred to her, wild and risky, but she knew the story she had to try to tell: their own. She took a steadying breath and squeezed Larkin's hand, earning a confused look from her friend. She didn't understand yet, but she would.

"Once, there was a place called the Glades, a swamp where humans and creatures lived side by side in harmony," she said, the words spilling from her. "There were ferocious dragon-gators with a sweet tooth, mischievous pix-squitoes, tricky marsh-maids, and more. And holding them together was the Labyrinth Tree at the center of it all."

She felt the Labyrinth Tree's heartbeat jump before beginning to slow, becoming steadier. She looked at Larkin and saw understanding light her hazel eyes.

"And for more than a decade, the Glades was peaceful," she said. "But when the king of the Glades died, the land fell into chaos. The people and the creatures grieved, and the grief became a curse."

"It's working," Larkin said, her voice barely louder than a whisper. Behind her, Cordelia could see Dash and Zephyr running toward them and while the roots hadn't gone completely still, they didn't try to grab at the boys as they ran.

"Dash!" Cordelia's mother called out from above.

"Zephyr!" Aunt Minerva added.

Both boys' eyes darted up to the canopy, searching, but they didn't stop running toward Cordelia and Larkin.

"Keep it going," Cordelia told Larkin, who nodded. Their

brothers joined them, out of breath and panting as they too wrapped their arms around the heart trunk.

"But in the middle of so much chaos, four children set off on a quest through the Glades in search of a witch who could bring the king back to life," Larkin said. "They faced many trials and troubles, but along the way they realized that a rot ran through their home, a rot that was strongest in its heart—in the Labyrinth Tree at its center."

The tree shuddered at that, recognizing its part in the story. Cordelia pressed on.

"When they finally made it to the witch's house, they found that she couldn't bring the king back after all."

"But it was okay," Dash added, looking between Cordelia and Larkin. "It was okay because the power to heal the Glades was within them."

Aunt Astrid appeared, running from the opposite direction as Dash and Zephyr, and now the roots had gone still. Not just still, Cordelia thought, but rapt, as if they too were hanging on every word of the story the children were spinning.

"Can you heal it?" Larkin asked Aunt Astrid, who held her hand to the tree. Her brow furrowed, but after a second, she gave a quick nod.

In the lapse of the story, the roots began to stir once more. "We have to keep telling the story," Cordelia said. "What happens next?"

The four children exchanged a look, but Zephyr was the one who spoke up. "The children had learned a lot of things from the king," he said, pausing to sniffle. "How to help those in need, how to listen, how to believe in themselves, and most of all, how to tell stories."

"Zephyr, I need your help," Aunt Astrid said, reaching out for Zephyr's hand and placing it with hers on the trunk.

"Should I sneeze?" Zephyr asked.

Aunt Astrid shook her head. "You have control of your power now, even without sneezing," she told him. "Just focus on the tree and the rot and imagine clearing it."

The tree writhed, as if rebelling against the magic Aunt Astrid and Zephyr were trying to wield. It needed to be distracted, Cordelia thought, like she did when she had to take a gross dose of medicine.

"They learned how to tell stories," Cordelia said, picking up where Zephyr had left off. "And the creatures of the Glades loved hearing them, but none more than the Labyrinth Tree."

"So they set off with the witch to find the heart trunk of the Labyrinth Tree, which had taken their parents," Larkin added, glancing up into the canopy, though it was so thick they couldn't see anything. Their parents had gone quiet, and Cordelia wondered if they could hear the story too, if they understood what was happening, if they trusted her and the others to fix this.

"And when they reached the heart trunk, they could feel the rot within it, the rot that oozed all through the Glades. In order to heal it, they had to work together to tell a story," Cordelia said.

"Their story," Dash added.

"*Our* story," Larkin corrected, giving Dash a small smile. She trailed off, her eyes widening upon seeing Aunt Astrid and Zephyr's hands. Cordelia followed her gaze to see a warm golden aura surrounding the trunk, but beneath the glow was a sticky black tar. As they all watched, the golden aura surrounded the black tar, glowing brighter and brighter until the black tar disappeared altogether, blasted away by the light.

Aunt Astrid and Zephyr lowered their hands and the golden glow faded away. Around them, the branches of the Labyrinth Tree gave a great shudder before several clumps of roots lowered, bringing Cordelia's mother and both of Larkin's parents along with it. All three of them looked disheveled, with messy hair and wrinkled clothes, though Cordelia wondered how much of that was due to the tree taking them prisoner and how much of it was because they'd spent days worrying over her and the others. It was a surprise to see Uncle Verne, who was often out on his fishing boat, but when he saw Larkin and Zephyr, his weatherbeaten face broke into a relieved grin. As soon as they were back on solid ground, Cordelia, Larkin, Dash, and Zephyr ran to them, hugging their parents tight. Cordelia's mother smoothed her hand over Cordelia's back, but she could feel the tremor there, see the worry still lingering in her mother's eyes.

"It's over," Cordelia told her mother, remembering what Aunt Astrid said about how afraid she'd been. "I'm sorry we left, I'm sorry you worried, but it's over now."

Her mother hugged her and Dash tighter and it took Cordelia a moment to register that her shoulder was wet, that her mother was crying, that Cordelia was crying too.

"I just wanted Dad back," Cordelia told her. "I didn't know . . . I *don't* know what to do without him."

Her mother pulled back, her eyes red from crying, and she brushed her hand over Cordelia's cheek, wiping away her own tears. "Neither do I," she admitted. "But we'll get through it. *Together.*"

"It isn't fair," Cordelia told her.

"It isn't," her mother agreed. "I wish he could see you now—he'd be proud. And I wish he could see you grow up. There's so much he had to teach you."

Dash took Cordelia's hand and squeezed it. "I can teach you to drive a fan boat," he told her before glancing at their mother, whose eyebrows were raised so high they nearly disappeared into her hairline. "Even if I'm not actually allowed," he added hastily.

Cordelia smiled softly. "And I'll teach you to make a bon-

fire, at least when I trust you won't burn down the village."
She looked at her mother. "Do you know what the secret
ingredient was in his redfish?"

Her mother bit her lip. "Grapefruit zest," she said, her
own voice gone thin and fragile. "He put grapefruit zest in
the marinade."

"Do you know how to shoot a bow and arrow?" Dash
asked her hopefully.

Their mother smiled, reaching down to ruffle his hair,
but her eyes darted over Dash's shoulder, to where Aunt
Astrid was standing, watching the reunions uncertainly.
"You'll have to ask Aunt Astrid that—she taught your father
everything he knew about bows and arrows. Maybe if you
ask nicely, she'll teach you too. When you're older."

Something Cordelia didn't fully understand passed between the two women, and Aunt Astrid gave a shaky nod.

"When you're older," she echoed. And then her mother
was hugging Aunt Astrid too, and so was Aunt Thalia, and
then they were all hugging—one big group. For a second,
Cordelia felt like her father was there too, holding them together.

"Let's go home," she said.

CHAPTER THIRTY-SIX

Cordelia, Larkin, and their brothers were grounded for a whole month when their mothers brought them back to the village, allowed to do nothing but go to school and come straight back home. Cordelia knew better than to protest the punishment—even she had to admit that running away into a wild swamp full of feral creatures was a big offense, though she argued that saving her mother, Aunt Minerva, and Uncle Verne from the angry Labyrinth Tree should have made up for it just a little.

She thought her father would be proud of her for breaking the curse, but more than that, Cordelia knew he *wouldn't* be proud of her for putting her mother through such a difficult couple of days.

Still, she couldn't bring herself to regret the journey she and her friends had taken, especially when it became clear that the swamp really *was* healing. There had been no more tales of stinging pix-squito swarms or mangrove roots trying to drown people or marsh-maids singing their luring songs. Even Quince had made a reappearance in the village the day after the Labyrinth Tree was healed, seeming to apologize to Larkin for her bad behavior. While Aunt Minerva and Uncle Verne put their feet down about Larkin keeping a dragon-gator for a pet, Quince had made herself at home on the riverbank closest to Larkin's house and followed her almost everywhere.

Aunt Astrid had moved in with Larkin's family while her cottage was being fixed, though Cordelia had a feeling that there was no rush on the project—Aunt Astrid seemed perfectly happy to be surrounded by loved ones again, and Larkin had told Cordelia that Aunt Astrid was helping with her and Zephyr's magic lessons. Cordelia suspected whatever tensions had caused the wedge between her and the others still existed, but when she asked her mother about it, she'd told her that their issues seemed smaller now, in the scope of things.

That was another effect of her father's death, Cordelia supposed. Loss and grief had a way of bringing people together. She thought her father would be happy to see it.

❦

When their grounding was finally over, Larkin and Zephyr slept over at Cordelia and Dash's. After Aunt Thalia had gone to sleep, Larkin and Cordelia stayed up, talking in their beds.

"Do you think what happened to Aunt Astrid and our parents might happen to us?" Cordelia asked her, whispering the question into the dark night.

Larkin rolled over to face her, propping her head up on her elbow. "I used to worry about that a lot," she admitted.

"Used to?" Cordelia asked, frowning.

"There doesn't seem to be much to worry about now," Larkin pointed out. "Aunt Astrid is living in our house, she spends most days with my parents and your mom. I think it's safe to say they're friends again."

"Only because my dad died," Cordelia countered.

Larkin thought about that for a moment. "Then we'll learn from their mistakes," she said. "We'll make the choice to stay friends, no matter what, even when you get angry and push me away because you don't want anyone to see that you're hurt."

Cordelia shook her head, though she knew Larkin was right—she did do that, and she would try not to. "And even when you get so caught up in being the world's best witch that you forget about me," she added softly.

Larkin went quiet. "Is that what you think?" she asked.

Cordelia shrugged. "It feels like we're heading in different directions, Lark," she said gently.

"We're different people," Larkin agreed. "But as long as we *want* to be friends, nothing can stop us. It's a choice. And I know that I'll always choose to be your friend."

Cordelia reached out toward Larkin, taking her hand and squeezing it tight. "And I'll always choose to be yours."

An hour later, Cordelia and Larkin woke their brothers and brought them up to the roof, just like Oziris had done after the winter solstice party. They sat beneath the stars, blankets wrapped around their shoulders, and stared up at the wide-open sky above.

"I wished for magic," Larkin said after a while, breaking the silence. When Cordelia and their brothers looked at her with frowns, she clarified. "During the star shower. When Oziris said to make a wish, that was what I wished for. It came true."

"Well, I wished not to have magic," Zephyr said. "That definitely didn't come true."

"But you only wished that because you couldn't control it," Cordelia pointed out. "That was what you really wanted, wasn't it?"

Zephyr considered this. "I guess," he said after a moment. "I do really like my magical boogers, now that I'm not worried about hurting someone with them."

"And, thankfully, according to Aunt Astrid, soon you won't *need* your boogers to use your magic—like you did with the tree the second time around."

"But I can still use them," Dash said with a grin. "When I want to."

Cordelia rolled her eyes. "What did you wish for, Dash?" she asked her brother.

"Candy," he said, and everyone laughed. Dash laughed too, even as his cheeks turned red. "I didn't realize it was supposed to be something deep and meaningful—I just wanted candy."

"Well, you always manage to find more candy, so your wish must have come true too," Zephyr told him.

"And you?" Larkin asked Cordelia. "What did you wish for?"

Cordelia swallowed, thinking back to that night, with her father's presence warm and comforting and the world full of unlimited possibilities—a prospect that had both thrilled and terrified her.

I wish everything could stay exactly like this, always.

Her wish hadn't come true. So much had changed from that night, but there were constants too—the world was still a large and wonderful and terrible place, and Cordelia knew that she was still loved, by her mother and Larkin and their brothers and her aunts and by her father too, even if he wasn't there anymore. She was still his daughter; that hadn't changed.

Not even death could take that away.

"I wished for this," she said after a moment, and vague as the words were, her friends didn't push her for more.

Cordelia closed her eyes and listened to the wind blow through the saw grass—the whispers of the dead, as her father had told her once. When she'd listened during the unmooring, she hadn't heard anything, but now she knew she hadn't really been listening. She hadn't been ready to.

Now she was.

I love you, she heard in the sound. *I love you. I love you. I love you.*

AUTHOR'S NOTE

Into the Glades is, of course, a work of fiction, but parts of it are inspired by my childhood growing up in the Florida Redlands, near the Everglades. Larkin, Cordelia, Zephyr, and Dash are fictional, though there are bits and pieces of myself, my brother, and our two childhood best friends in them. My brother Jerry's boogers were not magical, for example, but his reputation for notoriously booger-y sneezes has managed to follow him well into adulthood even if he has, like Zephyr, learned to better control them.

Oziris, too, is fictional, but his real-life counterpart was Steve Levine, my oldest friend's dad, who I'd known for as long as I could remember, and who died, suddenly, in a car accident when I was eleven. I remember him as a loving father who put his children above all else, an adventurous spirit who dared us to always reach for the impossible, and a world-class storyteller who was my gateway into the realm of fantasy books. More than twenty years after his passing, his death still strikes me as profoundly unfair. I believe, though, that he would be proud to see the adults his children, Madison and Jake, have grown into, and that his pride would extend to my brother and me as well, for the part he played in shaping us.

We remain, to this day and forevermore, his heathen children, causing a ruckus.

ACKNOWLEDGMENTS

While writing can often feel like a solitary pursuit, it is in fact a group effort, and *Into the Glades* wouldn't exist without the support of so many people. First, thank you to my wonderful agent, John Cusick, who helped me mold this book from the very first idea spark, and my editor, Hannah Hill, who fell in love with the Glades and its inhabitants as much as I did.

Thank you to everyone at Delacorte Press and Random House Children's Books, especially Beverly Horowitz, Barbara Marcus, and Krista Marino, for supporting me through this new branch of my career.

Thank you to Katherine Webber Tsang, Kevin Tsang, Elizabeth Eulberg, and Kamilla Benko for welcoming me to the land of writing for a younger audience, and for providing such wonderful advice and friendship along the way. And thank you to my wonderful network of other friends and loved ones: Cara and Alex Schaeffer, Sasha Alsberg, Jefrey Pollock, Deborah Brown, Isaac and Jesse Pollock, Catherine Chan, Alwyn Hamilton, Samantha Shannon, Julie

Scheurl, Lexi Wangler, and whoever I inevitably forgot this time around—I owe you a batch of cookies.

Thank you to my family: my dad, David; my stepmom, Denise; my brother, Jerry; and my sister-in-law Jill. And my other family, Madison, Jake, and Tracy. I'm so lucky to have all of you in my corner.

ABOUT THE AUTHOR

LAURA SEBASTIAN grew up in South Florida and attended Savannah College of Art and Design. She now lives and writes in London with her two dogs, Neville and Circe. Laura is the author of the *New York Times* bestselling young adult series The Ash Princess and *Castles in Their Bones,* as well as *Half Sick of Shadows,* her first novel for adults.

laurasebastianwrites.com